THE SHACKLE

"THIS WILL LAST AS LONG AS YOU LIKE AND NO LONGER . . ." I accept my new condition with interested curiosity. I content myself with what satisfies other women in my position, the free time he procures me by going out.

Realize this, you who say you love me: the most loving mistress turns away from her lover during certain hours which she mysteriously arranges and which she cherishes in anticipation. The most beautiful woman, if you perpetually spy on her, will not survive undamaged. The most faithful one needs to hide herself, if only to be able to think freely . . .

Also by Colette
Published by Ballantine Books:

THE VAGABOND

Colette

THE
SHACKLE

Translated by
Antonia White

BALLANTINE BOOKS · NEW YORK

ISBN 0-345-30058-0

First Ballantine Books Edition: July 1982

{1}

IT IS NOT THE CALM CIRCLE OF LIGHT THROWN BY A lamp lit every night on the same table that shows a woman what little she can perceive of herself: yet by changing the table, the lamp and the room, what have I acquired? Only the suspicion, soon to become a certainty, that all countries are going to be exactly alike unless I find the secret of making them new again by renewing my own self. I can no longer rely on my sturdy reason—the sturdy reason of a woman! At the moment she is feeling neither sturdy nor reasonable, but very tremulous and emotional—all because of a trivial encounter on the Promenade des Anglais.

Yet it was so obvious that it was bound to happen sooner or later; it was amazing it had not happened before. Here he was, right beside me, the man who had wanted to give me his name, his love, the support of his steady heart. And he passed by without even seeing me. On one side of him he had a young woman; on the other a very small, plump child who could barely walk. He did not see me because he was giving his entire attention—his touching, slightly owlish attention—to the stumbling child. "Big Booby!" He passed so close that I could see his long, stiff eyelashes and his tie knotted as if he had knotted it for life. He was so like himself that I could have put out my hand, just as in the old days, to loosen that tie a little and thrust the too visible corner of a handkerchief further down into his jacket pocket. It frightens me now to think of the gesture I might have made. He was so utterly unaware of me that I had the impression of being no longer a

1

living person but an insubstantial ghost he was going to walk right through. It is odd that I did not think of looking at his wife and child. All three of them continued their stroll along the sea front.

What has shaken me so much? Not love, not grief. How much does regret account for my disturbance? I have no idea. The shock, the flash of revelation have just made me far more aware of my frailty than the insane daily reverie in which I delude myself I am wise. Call it meditation, if you like. There is no such thing as wise meditation. All habitual meditation contains a germ of delirium. It borders on hysteria, on artificially-induced ecstasy, painful or otherwise.

And there I go, generalising in a typically feminine way. So much the better! There are moments like this when I am quite glad to find myself reacting like a female. It is as if I were establishing the fact that I may still be good for something—from the sexual point of view.

Would I have liked him to see me? No, not really. I repeat his name, his cumbersome name, uneasily: Maxime Dufferein-Chautel . . . I am sure I do not love him. But all the same, that man represents love in my life. Not only love, but adventure, even sensual pleasure. No doubt that is what is keeping me in a tremor and feeling vaguely shocked. That mouth, those hands, that great warm body—all those things taken together very nearly constituted a lover for me three years ago. If he had been alone, just now, and had spoken to me, should I have called him Max, or "darling" or just "you"? He had on his most married look, but that, if I may presume to say so, is a look he was born with. He was displaying that wife and child of his as if they were new purchases he had just made in the Place Masséna.

Let me try to be sincere. I did not fly from him, but I hid myself in the only way that could conceal me from his eyes, in complete immobility; the startled hare squats close to the ground and knows perfectly well that it is the colour of a ploughed furrow. The slightest flutter of my white glove against my dark dress would have attracted his eye; I even dreaded that my scent, still the same scent, might suddenly make him turn round. I did not want him to, no, I did not want him to. I blushed like a woman caught with her hair in curl-papers. And, besides, *he* had such an air of wealth, of having acquired so many new things: a brand-new child, a befurred and befeathered wife, a walking-stick I did not recognise; whereas *I!* He humiliated me with his air of having made a fortune. I had nothing to show him but a tailored suit, and, naturally, a pretty hat, and a slightly different way of doing my hair. Perhaps he would have looked for something new on me and about me, with an expression of disappointment: "It that all?"

I felt, yes, I did feel as self-conscious as a poor person. This year, in Nice, he would not have seen the big orange and black posters announcing the appearance of Renée Néré, because Renée Néré is not "touring" any more. If he had asked what I was doing, I should have had to tell him that I had become a lady of leisure. A lady of leisure, living on a small private income; neither rich nor poor—not young, but not old either; not happy, but not depressed. Tonight, something comes back to me—something Brague said in one of his sallies.

"One never looks anything but what one is. Therefore, even when I am well-dressed, *I* look like . . . precisely, I look like a great actor. Whereas *you* don't look like a great actress, nor like a little one. Neither do you look like a 'lady'. Or a tart. You have an air—so—of folding your paws under you because the world disgusts you, but that's no indication. The fact is you go through life like those customers who don't know what they want to buy in a shop, those women the people behind the counter are longing to kick in the arse all the time they're saying politely: 'Take your time, Madam: have a good look round before you make up your mind.' Real swine of customers, you know!"

He laughed, and, to please him, I pretended to be very indignant.

*   *   *

At the end of a cloudless day, it is raining. The Promenade des Anglais glistens and the noise of the shower on the palm-trees and on the pavement drowns the rhythmic murmur of the sea. Where is the couple that went by at three o'clock, in front of the hotel, bending over the small child all in white? They cannot live here. I can picture them better on the outskirts of Cannes, in a villa surrounded by a garden, like the rich, respectable bourgeois they are. They must have come into Nice to have tea, in a comfortable closed limousine, with Baby on their knees. He must have married in haste, that man who was my friend, very nearly my lover, since his child is already walking. He cannot have lamented for long over the letter I left him one cold, grey spring morning: "My darling Max, I am going away . . ." Well! I'm obviously fated to think of nothing else tonight and there's no great harm in that.

True, I didn't look at his wife but now I can see their group again in all its details. A young woman, of the type people probably think pretty when they get to know her. She struck me as someone who went about absentmindedly, with an irresponsible, slightly cowlike placidity. "Ask my husband. . . ." And I'm prepared to bet "my husband" deals with everything, from Baby's nurse, to the chauffeur waiting for orders. He opens the laundry book every Monday morning and flattens down the page with the palm of his big brown hand; he confers with the cook. Perhaps there are days when he remembers me and those days he orders "pork cutlets in sauce, with gherkins". Perhaps, sometimes, his young wife calls him "Max"—in a voice he thinks he recognises, and, if he makes her laugh, she may happen to shrug her shoulders and say "Big booby!" When she does that, he must lean his head against her and close his eyes so as to hide two things, a flicker of emotion and the perverse pleasure of lying without saying a word, the pleasure all men savour when they subtly deceive us at the moment they are most passionately embracing us.

There I am, off again. Guessing, or inventing. Penetrating, thanks to my memories, my former lover's new marital life. I am probing it with all the spiteful curiosity of an abandoned mistress, whereas, on the contrary, it was I who . . . Worse still, I am using the erotic and varied imagination of the chaste, reinforced by an all too precise memory. I am raising—and by what right?—a ghost between Max and his wife; the ghost of an unforgotten, unforgettable Renée Néré. Unforgettable, no! But I ask you, in what way am I better than that cold, lovely blockhead of a Villepreux, the singer who used to sigh every time she heard a man's name mentioned: "Poor fellow! He's mad about me . . . he tried to kill himself . . . he's gone into exile . . ."? At least Villepreux, faithful to her illusions, enjoyed the rich satisfaction of lunatics in padded cells who believe they are reincarnations of Jesus Christ or Napoleon Bonaparte.

It is raining harder then ever. I shall not leave my room again. Yet tonight the posters of the Eldorado display the name of one of my ex-colleagues in the music-hall world: I would have liked to have gone round behind and had a word with her in her dressing-room, given her a surprise. I shan't go. The nearest lighthouse is drawing a neat little silver paintbrush over the rainy sea. I have taken my hair down while I was watching the beam and, instead of leaving it loose for the night, here I am mechanically putting it up again in the way I did it three years ago, pulled down in tufts over my ears and rolled on my nape to give the effect of a medieval page's curled locks. Have I aged? Yes, no, yes and no. Something in the colour and texture of my face reminds me of the distinguished, parched look that is the penalty of women who have to restrict liquid to a minimum in their diet. I no longer like this heavy, pulled-down curtain of hair. Nowadays I show the "fresh areas" that have not often been exposed to the light: ears, temples, a triangle of forehead, the nape of the neck. As to the hollow of my back, the upper part of my arms and chest, I cannot yet bring myself to uncover them, as Brague used to say "in mufti". The skin of one's arms and legs, the roundness of one's breasts, is a kind of fabric one exhibits on the stage, and only on the stage, covered with a sticky foundation that holds the powder; a cold fabric offered from a distance, out of reach of hands or lips; merely a rather striking part of one's costume. And I have noticed it over and over again in actresses I have played with in the theatre or on the music-halls—this curious, professional distortion of the sense of modesty which allows them to face the glare of the footlights naked, with perfect confidence, but forbids them to appear off the stage except behind ramparts of stiff, severe silk and opaque lace.

Although it is a year since I left the theatre my decorum remains strictly professional, and I hide this, that and the other which people might well envy me. The beautiful dancer Bastienne, a superb, placid, nymph-like creature, also used to insist on her dressmaker putting a triple layer of ninon in the neck of a dinner dress. She used to say, slapping her rigidly corseted breasts, "all *that* only concerns my job and my lover!"

I no longer have a job . . . and I have no lover. Nevertheless this afternoon's encounter made me put on that dress again for dinner just now, as if out of defiance—that black dress I did not dare wear, almost a real "low-cut" dress that reveals such a wide, deep triangle of white neck. Stiff with nervousness, my teeth clenched, I walked heroically to my little table at the far end, well away from the gypsy band—and no one paid any attention either to my dress or to me. Was I expecting Max—"Monsieur Dufferein-Chautel and family"—to dine at the Hôtel Impérial? Honestly no one, except the inevitable gentleman-on-his-own who is interested in the lady-on-her-own, follows her about for a few days, tries to make her acquaintance, succeeds or does not succeed—and goes off.

As a lady-on-her-own, in fact a positively classic type of lady-on-her-own, with dresses a little too respectable for my kind of face, it was impossible for me to avoid the gentleman-on-his-own. I have had one for the past week. I could not describe him, for I have not seen him. When I look at the spot where he is, it is not him that I see; I see through him as if through an empty water-jug. I only know the shape of his back, because he promptly turns away from me with an affec-

tation of politeness. Seen from the front, he is a
stranger; I can only distinguish him from the others
when he turns his back to me. It is at mealtimes he
embarrasses me most because I can *hear* him thinking
about me while he is eating. Tonight, yielding to that
vaguely amorous will, I smiled at him, with my
thoughts on Max. I ought not to have done it. But it's
so utterly unimportant!

The rain has stopped lashing the windows and the
silence wakes me up again. Silence, here, is the sputter
of the short waves as they dissolve on the pebbles, the
trot of the lively little hoofs of a countryman's horse,
the hooting of car-horns. I open the window and lean
out to see two lighted windows on the floor below: my
friend May's room. Shadows pass over the curtains.
There are two tempestuous lovers down there for
whom a quarrel, followed by fisticuffs, constitutes a
kind of Swedish gymnastics. If I went down to them,
they would not stop for such a trifling interruption. I
could sit down and score the hits until the disturbing,
ferocious moment, when, both covered with bruises,
these peculiar lovers can think of no better punishment
for each other than a passionate embrace.

Or else I might climb up two floors where, behind
another white door. I should find the stifling, scented
room of two other nomad friends. Wherever these two
go, they take their opium lamp, their flat cushions
which smell of precious wood and their white Indian
mat, smooth and cold as a lizard's skin. There, too, I
could sit down, as a spectator, or lie down and share,
not the poison I keep away from, but the warm silence,
the air heavy with the dark aroma, the slightly halluci-
nated repose.

Above and below, I should be welcome—someone
who takes nothing from and gives nothing to anyone.
Ah! I have no illusions, either, about what I receive
from my *friends*. Not a cadger, but not a giver, that's
what they must say of me. And what could I give? It
is true that a woman who obstinately refuses to sleep
with anyone always seems miserly, whatever she does.
My "friends", idlers of the Riviera, flotsam and jetsam

of the theatre world, easily-shocked illicit couples who value my good behaviour, deny me what they readily grant to May: that vaguely contemptuous trust, that affectionate covetousness which she maintains and satisfies with a coarse love-word and a crude gesture that her childish laugh robs of offence.

On the floor above, on the floor below, the same gay welcome awaits me. But when I get up to go back to my room—157—my departure will distress nobody, either upstairs or down. I can come and go as I like, do whatever I fancy. Only, as a little girl said: "I haven't got a fancy." So I shall go to bed, but not at once, because the air is so good to breathe, still all damp. It smells of gardens and sea-shells. There is a young moon over the sea, a slender moon that sheds no light.

After all, it is a pleasant enough thing, just because of an emotional encounter, or the clear, scented interval between two showers or for nothing, for no reason at all, to feel a little foolish and agitated and weak, to feel oneself melting all over like a young girl who has just received her first love-letter.

[2]

"So then?"

"So it went on like that till three in the morning. At three o'clock, grand beating-up. Six hundred francs worth of tortoise-shell hairpins left on the carpet!"

"Ah! And after that?"

"After that, naturally . . . I'm sleepy."

May laughed and stretched. She had just come up to my room, wearing only a Roumanian shirt under her Japanese kimono, her bare feet thrust into large man's slippers. She radiated a perishable, impersonal freshness. May has no features and immensely thick hair of unequal degrees of fairness; light on the nape of her neck, silvery on the temples, elsewhere almost brown. Twenty-five! What a waste of precious youth! Anyone would think this vehement creature had sworn to ruin her looks before she was thirty: the tips of her long eyelashes are discoloured with mascara and her beautiful hair is daily scorched with hot tongs. May never goes to bed, forgets to eat lunch, smokes, drinks and takes cocaine. But what does it matter? In spite of it all the absurd little thing has the clear skin of a twenty-five year old blonde, horse-chestnut coloured eyes whose irises leave hardly any space for the whites and a charming, imbecile way of exaggerating fashions which are crazy enough already.

She goes off in the morning—the "morning" being between twelve-thirty p.m. and four o'clock—in broadly-striped skirts that reveal her stubby, tortured little feet, her ankles and even her calves; the waistline is somewhere under her armpits, defined by the edge of a tight, skimpy little jacket which never did look as if it had been cut for May and which, in front, shows the little potbelly she has recently acquired. A cascade of soft linen opens on to the parting between her breasts and a straw helmet conceals her right eye. Such is the outfit which May calls "ever such a simple little run-about suit".

I have known May for over a year—from eternity according to her—through having met her at a night-club where Brague and I were performing as honest wage-earners. She was having supper at the next table and behaved outrageously to make an impression on me. She laughed, dipped her hair in the champagne, displayed the rudeness of a child and the cynicism of a young Negress, wept deliciously for no reason, threw coins into the bodice of a Spanish dancer and ruined everything by those simple words: "I'm a real character, aren't I?"

The "real character" walked to and fro in front of my dressing-table, cutting off the sunlight every other instant with the fluttering shadow of her huge sleeves. Dazzled, I powdered my face as best I could. If May trails about in her lover's slippers which make her feet look like Little Tich's, it is neither by mistake nor out of carelessness; it is "to shock the old fogeys in the corridors".

"Look at that," she said abruptly, thrusting her downy arm under my nose. "That'll be black tomorrow."

I examined, with the proper interest, two yellowish-brown bruises circling each of May's arms like bracelets.

"The filthy brute!" she muttered, not without deference. "And, you know, he ruined my dress, a dress that cost fifty louis—all because I felt in a lucky mood and I wanted to go and play at Monte Carlo. He's going to find out what it costs him, that dress! I've already played one good trick on him before I came up!"

"Now, now May, no details!"

"Don't worry, it's not what you think. I took advantage of him being asleep to pull a hair out of his nose. You ought to have heard the yell the brute gave—I

thought the porter was going to come up! Do you think
that made him get out of bed? He went straight back
to sleep! There he is, flat on his back in that purple
nightshirt like a tart's, and he said he wouldn't get up
unless you came and pulled him out by his feet."

It is almost impossible for me to avoid knowing the
most intimate details of May's domestic life. She has
such a crude, vivid way of describing her lover to me
that I know how that man washes, goes to sleep and
wakes up, and May does not restrict herself to information of that kind. However, today, I was not interested
in smutty talk.

"And what about lunch?"

"What lunch?" yawned May. The little tongue that
showed between the shining teeth was not moist enough
and was white in the middle.

"Why, ours of course! You wanted us to lunch together. Well, it's a quarter to one and you've got no
further than putting on *his* bedroom slippers! So whatever time are we going to have lunch?"

May planted herself in front of the window with her
legs and arms outspread in the shape of an X; her
cloudy hair looked as if it was smoking in the sunlight.

"What time? How on earth do I know? This woman
never talks about anything else; the time it is, the time
it's going to be, the time it ought to be! One lunches
when one feels like it, one goes to bed when one feels
like it—— Time's only for flunkeys and station-masters!
That's what I say. Oh my, what a face! Listen—because it's you—I'll just dash upstairs to the others. If
they're chockful of the drug, I'll leave them and come
haring down again and wake my man up with a good
glass of Vittel water—nice and cold—delicately poured
over all his most sensitive spots. After that, thirty-five
minutes and I'm ready! Oh, you make me sick, the
whole lot of you! By the way, would you like me to
get the hors-d'œuvre sent up to you?"

She departed in calculated disorder, slithering about
in her man's slippers, catching her Japanese sleeves on
the door-key.

*   *   *

What a beautiful Riviera day lies in front of me and
below me! As yesterday, this noonday hour in Nice
gives us all it can; sunshine that prevents one from
thinking or taking action and a summer breeze. There
are two sails slanting over the sea and, above the sea,
a distant aeroplane. The road, freshly sprinkled, makes
a dark track, restful to the eyes. There is no traffic on
it but the long motor-cars that dart past like fishes and
the slow horse-drawn cabs with their drivers chewing
a sprig of mimosa. Beyond, the blinding white Promenade is thronged with strollers and dogs on leads.
There are hardly any children in the crowd. You could
easily count the little bare legs running about or the
uncertainly toddling bundles of snowy lace and batiste
like that one yesterday. Nice is a town for grown-up
people.

My eye is caught by vivid hats, by the fresh, acid
green of a passing dress. I can see immaculate costumes
of light, far too light silk. They make me think of those
butterflies which the first treacherous rays of spring
lure to their death. Alongside them, I can see women
heavily swathed in furs and, sitting on the benches,
prudent strollers armed with green umbrellas and
woollen shawls. I am reminded of those restaurants
where the headwaiter offers you a fan while the page-
boy slips a hot-water bottle under your feet.

In front of the hotel, mandolines and Italian singers
make a musical buzzing that the wind carries away in
gusts, and I think I can smell something slightly sicken-
ing to my famished stomach, the scent of flat straw
baskets loaded with violets and red carnations.

When are we going to have lunch? Down below, on
the jetty, a fox-terrier whose barking is so continuous
that one does not notice it keeps obstinately trying to
bring back a pebble too big for him as a souvenir of
the beach. That is the fiftieth time a red hat, encircled
by a green cord fastened with a purple rosette has gone
by. And how many times have I counted the return of
those two short-skirted young women—less chic ver-
sions of May—one in green, the other in yellow, teeter-
ing along with tiny, painful steps on their absurd heels?
They do not go far; in any case, you would think that,

some five hundred yards away, there is an invisible barrier which nearly all the strollers come up against and which forces them to turn back. Yet, further on, there is a fine, tempting stretch where one can step out and hear the sound of the sea.

I am also gazing at a bright little restaurant, moored to the edge of the Promenade like a house-boat. Brague and I used to lunch there in the old days; silent, contented, stupefied with sunshine . . . I'm hungry. My friends will quite likely be another hour. As to the two above, I don't expect them.

The two down below will arrive quarrelling; she with that perfume which is so strong as to be slightly pharmaceutical; he well-scrubbed, with his hair damp and his hand warm from his bath. And they will exchange insults or kisses that smell of mouth-wash. Their quarrels and their caresses which demand neither darkness nor privacy will continue until lunch, for we *shall* have lunch. Oh yes, we shall end up lunching in the almost-empty room that will smell of cold fried food, the onions of the hors d'œuvre, and tangerines. We shall lunch in spite of the indefatigable gypsy band, in spite of May's contradictory orders to the head-waiter.

By the time they pour out our coffee, the four o'clock sun will be reddening over the sea. Then we shall set off in the car for "a little outing for the good of our health" through a glacial, mauve twilight. Round about seven, May, shivering and bad-tempered, will demand her tea at Cap Martin, and I shall have seen yet another beautiful day crumble away goodness knows how, useless, shrunk to nothing and ruined.

> *Bonsoir, Madame la Lune,*
> *Bonsoir!*
> *C'est votre ami Pierrot qui vient vous voir.*

May sings in tune, but, in my opinion, the planet's rising could well have done without the Montmartre serenade. The moon rising over the sea, the red misty moon, not yet full, was the same slender one that had sailed between two clouds the other night when I had given up trying to go to sleep. The brief, anguished awareness of time flying by so fast, empty, made me all the more sensitive to the chilly hour. It was still daylight, but the light was withdrawing from the clumps of trees and even from the dusty verges of the road. The last vestiges clung obstinately to the white facades of buildings, to the winding road, to our own pale cheeks. It was that fugitive moment when one becomes aware, underneath the clustered villas and the artificial gardens, of the rather depressing and austere aridity of this rocky coast. Why did May have to sing *Bonsoir, Madame la Lune?*

There were four of us in the hired car that was bringing us back to Nice; May and myself in the back; Jean, her lover, and Masseau on the pull-down seats. As a keen wind was blowing our own dust, as well as that of the cars we passed, back in our faces, we were all of us half-masked with goggles. Now that May had woken me up, I amused myself by studying these three half-faces. The twilight hid the eyes behind a glitter of glass, but mouth, chin and nostrils became all the more eloquent. Had I not been masked myself, I would have been embarrassed by watching only the lips of the people to whom I was talking.

May suffered most under the mask with its big oval lenses: you realised that she had hardly any nose. Yet how young and mobile her rather flat mouth is! Looking at her full cheeks whose rich down holds the powder so well, I worried about my own slightly dried-up mask. But a yawn from Jean, May's Jean, suddenly interested me in this masculine face. I had never noticed before how the clean-shaven, sulky mouth, full-lipped but finely chiselled at the corners, revealed both the weaknesses and charms of his character, nor that the chin was at once obstinate and feminine, nor that the neck showing above the low collar was strong but so smoothly rounded that no muscles were visible. I decided that, when he removed his mask, I must take a better look at his eyes.

Masseau, of course, had been smoking opium the night before. You had only to look at the bad colour of his wry, sad, intelligent lips and the swelling on the lower part of his green cheeks between the big nose and the old-fashioned pointed beard. He was silent, waiting. Waiting to get back to Nice and smoke. He had made a slight, nervous grimace when May had started singing *Bonsoir, Madame la Lune,* and I thought—though I was not quite sure—that an extremely malicious smile had hovered on Jean's lips at the same moment.

Instinctively, I kept my mouth tight shut. I had all too good reason to fear that, with my eyes no longer there to give it the lie, people might read my real feelings on it; weariness, disgust at a day badly begun, spent in meaningless activity and ending up in our sullen silence.

The car in which we were travelling was not a particularly good one and the road itself anything but comfortable. Its rough, twisting course flung us now to the left, now to the right; I had to keep myself rigid to avoid collapsing on May and May kept flopping on to my shoulder. Our intellectual conversation was restricted to exclamations that were meant to be gay or that deplored the state of the roads. The lights of Monte Carlo wrenched a sigh from me; more than fifty minutes' drive ahead!

The lights woke May up. She removed her goggles, revealing her beautiful, blinking eyes and her scrap of a nose barred with a red groove.

"Jean! Jean! Suppose we stop and have dinner at Monte Carlo? Just as we are, all disgustingly filthy and messy? No? Why not? Oh, of course, as soon as I want to do something a bit amusing, I can't find a soul to back me up. Jean, look at the place where you hit me last year. Yes, dear, that's what he did to me, the brute! Jean, did you see that little villa on the corner, the Gonzalez's villa? Must be ruinous to rent a place like that in Monte Carlo!"

I too was reviving old memories as we drove through, but in silence. There was the Villa des Bananiers, a mediocre hotel for modest purses, where Brague and I used to put up along with other stage people, old women gamblers in black lace mantles and dowdy foreigners. Just by the Théâtre des Beaux-Arts, I know a shady and agreeable little English pub where

I used to drink scalding lemonade or velvety hot grog after the daily matinées. Round about five o'clock, I only met one Englishman there, patiently getting drunk. He had a dark red face, burnished by heavy drinking, and he used to hum a quavering little song. I can conjure it up so vividly—it's still all so close to me—the smell of hot canvas and damp earth that triumphed over the smell of grease-paint in the striped tents where we used to dress, at the Beaux-Arts, on those hot afternoons.

In front of the Hôtel de Paris, the car slowed down and hesitated, as if inviting us to get out.

"Jean, I tell you we ought to dine here."

The masked man shook his head, then changed his mind and turned his expressive half-face to me.

"Do you want to?"

"Oh! don't ask *me!*"

I wanted to return to Nice but, if I admitted it, I should start May off and, like a coward, I recoiled at the thought of three-quarters-of-an-hour of insults and tears.

"You know *I . . .*"

"I know," said Jean peremptorily. "Drive on, chauffeur, we're returning to Nice."

"Idiot," squeaked May into the wind. "It wouldn't have hurt you to be nice to me for once, would it? May I ask why you didn't want to stay and have dinner here?"

"Because I didn't feel like it," said Jean placidly.

A rusty laugh greeted this reply. It came from Masseau, who had not uttered a word for hours.

"Oh, so *you've* come to life!" May snapped at him aggressively. "Seems you're feeling better, then?"

Masseau removed his goggles and the passing lights played on his small, red-rimmed eyes. They were blinking and satanic, the eyes of a demon bureaucrat.

"I feel better, certainly, than if I were feeling worse. For if you say: 'I am feeling better', you appear to imply that at some previous, though unspecified period, you were feeling worse. However, since in general I am dissatisfied with my state of health, I can only reply:

Yes, I am feeling better, better than if I were feeling worse."

He has an old man's voice and an ageless face. He is frail, but only rarely tired; capriciously doped or prostrated by the "drug". May addresses him as "tu"— but she does that to so many men—yet she does not seem to know him any better than I do who have met him fourteen or fifteen times in a fortnight. When I questioned her once about Masseau, she replied: "Don't ask *me!* He's just an old chap, a colonial."

Now, revived by the darkness and the anticipation of the poison, he was waking up from his long and lugubrious muteness. He put up a fine-boned yellow hand, stroked the little goatee that looked like dried hay and said, glancing sidelong at me, "The gesture of the ladies' man."

He spread out his beard fanwise and said, "Henri IV."

He removed his soft hat, twisted a lock of hair into a horn above his forehead and said, *"Louis Dix,* the Headstrong."

Then he relapsed into his silence and his shivering, huddled immobility until the night, blacker after the lights of Monte Carlo, enveloped us again. The head-lamps that had just been switched on opened a tunnel of brightness in front of us, ringed with a pale, quivering rainbow. The dry, less chilly air expanded my nostrils and I leant the nape of my neck against the fold of the lowered hood with the relaxed, secure feeling that came from knowing that, till we reached Nice, I was invisible; the darkness veiled me better than my glass-eyed mask.

"Sorry," said the voice of Jean, whose knees had just brushed against mine.

"That's right, go on!" May reproached him. "Play footie-footie with her, that would be just the end!"

"Why 'the end'? You're not very polite to Madame Renée Néré, May!"

"What," murmured the voice of Masseau on the breeze, "is the end of the non-dining in Monte Carlo? Answer: the end of the non-dining in Monte Carlo is to play footie-footie with Madame Renée Néré."

I could feel May fidgeting with exasperation beside me.

"You're both too disgusting for words! To think I'm supposed to have an intelligent lover and that there are people cracked enough to say Masseau's got a distinguished mind! Honest, I'm still wondering what's so special about you and him! When did you last see yourself, you intelligent lover you, trying to do something to please me and putting yourself out for me?"

"Never," replied the intelligent lover very emphatically. "You're not an old lady and you're not one of my relatives. Consequently . . ."

Once again I was amused and dumbfounded by this couple in which the woman was treated *as* a woman only in bed.

Upright, May finds all the prerogatives of her sex withdrawn from her and the harmony of lovers transformed into school children's rivalries. People like that are new to me. I endured my husband's tyranny when I was a young and silly bride and Maxime Dufferein-Chautel would have liked to impose a tender, traditional middle-class authority upon me. I have seen my old friend Hamond submit to the lunatic caprices of an imperious child and, backstage, I have seen the primitive fervour which prostrates the female before a tribal chieftain. But never have I anywhere seen anything resembling May and Jean.

Apart from money, apart from love-making—if even in that!—she receives nothing from him in the way of masculine homage.

"What's more," May said suddenly, as if she had read my thoughts, "as from tomorrow morning, I'm taking a room and a bathroom for myself at the Impérial. I've had enough of you always bagging the first bath and finding a shaving-brush full of soap stuck beside my tooth-brush. My dear"—May turned her small face, which I could only make out as a pale blur, towards me—"I don't know if you're like me . . ."

"No," said Jean.

"What d'you mean, no?"

"I say: no, she's not like you. She doesn't find a

shaving-brush stuck beside her tooth-brush. Moreover, she isn't my mistress."

"Say you wish she were. Go on, say it at once!"

"Oh, why at once? May, when are you going to stop being in such a violent hurry? Always this haste that ruins all the best things in life! Why, only yesterday morning, to quote only one example . . ."

"Yesterday morning? What did I do, yesterday morning?"

"Do you want me to tell?"

Masseau, who had appeared to be asleep, became interested. As we passed through the lights of Beaulieu, he assumed, in order to listen, the dreamy pose of a sentimental "portrait-study" by Disderi. With one finger at the corner of his mouth, and his eyes and ears agog, he announced, "I am the Empress Eugénie."

But he was not destined to hear any scandalous revelations, for May provided a few peaceful passersby in Beaulieu with the unwonted spectacle of a young woman standing up in an open red car, scientifically boxing with a gentleman sitting opposite her and screaming at him: "I forbid you! I absolutely forbid you to tell about yesterday morning. Otherwise I'll tell you about your boil above your thigh and the story of the cotton-wool!"

These words produced a smart blow that sent her sprawling on to the back seat where I was keeping out of the way as best I could. I was thoroughly exasperated. This return by night, along the sea swept by horizontal luminous trails, could have been charming. The night had come on so quickly that one could hardly divine the black water rippling under the flotilla of lights and almost imperceptibly rocking it. The two lovers, originally locked together in combat, were still carrying on some kind of tussle. It was Masseau's obvious interest in it, rather than prudishness, that made me avert my head.

At last we were getting near Nice. That garland of living flame ahead of us was the Promenade des Anglais, and there on the Promenade was my temporary refuge, admittedly only an hotel bedroom, but at

least somewhere where I could lock the door behind
me, where I could smell my own perfume.

"What time is it?"

The question had burst out in spite of myself, as we
were passing the minute theatre whose name in red
electric bulbs lights up the last trees of the Jardin
Public. Such a tiny theatre! How cosy it was in there,
last year, while the December showers lashed the pavement and the leaves of the mimosas drooped like be-
draggled feathers!

"Pay a forfeit!" cried May. "She's asked the time,
she can't get away with less than a louis!"

"Paid to whom?" demanded Masseau.

The motor drew up in front of the entrance to the
Impérial, but May was too astonished to get out at
once.

"To whom? Why, me of course. When I'm about,
who else do you expect people to pay money to?"

Jean shrugged his shoulders and leapt out without
a word. No remark, however stinging, no cane, however supple, is capable of curing May of her inborn
defect: she scrounges and sponges, and, when she returns from a banquet, she does not exclaim: "There
were avalanches of flowers and fruit on the table!" but
estimates their cost precisely. "Peaches at five francs
apiece, my dears, and fifty louis' worth of orchids on
the table." May makes use of other people's purses, not
like a sponger but like a distinguished guest who must
be served first with every dish.

Ah, there we were at last! We had got back. Once
again, we had got back. Here we were again, capari-
soned in furs and goggled like Arctic explorers, after
having driven sixty miles along the Corniche. We stood
blinking in the white vestibule under the stares of the
English bachelors with their short pipes and of the
roulette players—twenty sous on the 5, twenty on the
10, and . . . hard luck! twenty sous on the 40 that
never turns up—all of whom had had their dinner
punctually and left the dining-room. Nevertheless, it
was for this unappreciative audience that May snatched
off her chinchilla cap and shook out her hair, releasing
a snow-storm of hairpins and Jean rewarded her with

a sharp surreptitious kick on the shin. Masseau, indifferent to fashion and even to good manners, yawned
so violently that tears came into his eyes, his goatee
thrust up by the extraordinary Medici collar of his
antique caped Ulster that looked like a German pro-
fessor's.

He caught sight of himself in a glass, pinched the
corners of his lips in an affected smile and, leaning
towards me, said confidentially, "Henri Trois."

The lift seemed a long while coming. I felt slightly
shamed at being subjected to the curiosity of these
strangers who were dividing up our group according
to their fancy and speculating: "Which of the two men
is the younger woman going up with?"

Finally the cage carried off all four of us, thus putting an end to a moment of general uneasiness, of false
intimacy, almost antipathy. We said: "See you later"
firmly and coldly as if we had no intention of meeting
again.

"Oh! those people, those people!" I can find nothing
to add, so I repeat once more: "Oh! those people! I've
had enough of them!"

The waiter who brought me a tray of tea and a
macedoine of fruit has gone off with a brief note of
excuse to May.

*"May dear, I must have caught a chill. I don't feel
at all well so shan't have dinner, but go straight to bed.
So sorry. See you tomorrow."*

Now, with my door locked and bolted, I can go on
pacing to and fro and working up my bad temper.
"I'm sick of those people!" A scalding, aromatic bath
which awaits me exhales its pungent steam. I am trailing
about in old bedroom slippers and my dressing-gown
gapes open over a crumpled chemise, whose slotted
insertion is empty of ribbon; it is only too obvious that
I put up meekly with the disastrous laundering one
gets in hotels. In the days when I earned my own
living, humbler lingerie never lacked ribbons or but-

tons. "Oh, *how* sick of those people I am!" But I name no names, for fear of accusing myself.

How can I blame Masseau, that cultured bibliomaniac, foundering in opium? Why accuse May, any more than Jean, of hooking on to me, when they only seek me out because I am as idle as they are? She is not spiteful and he is quite pleasant, a cautious man who laughs a great deal and never talks. Among the number of "those people" of whom I am so heartily sick ought I to include my poor Gentleman-on-his-own, and the staff of the hotel, and the strollers on the jetty? Yes, I prefer to. It's wiser—and less unjust. Poor May, who's done me no harm. . . . At this moment, she is dining with Jean at the Bonne Hôtesse or the Casino, or else Room 82 is resounding with the shrieks and blows of another "grand beating-up".

As I stretched my limbs and relaxed in my scalding-hot bath, I laughed unkindly imagining the May of tomorrow morning, battered and mercenary: "My dear, just look if he hasn't given me fifty louis' worth of bruises!"

Yes, I've had enough of those people, it's true. But, besides beginning to know myself, I am also beginning to know the advantages and disadvantages of this extraordinary part of the world where the mornings are enchanting and the nights, however starry, make one shiver in the discomfort of a double climate. Here cold nights are not invigorating and warm nights throb with fever rather than with passion. Have I, in so few days, become acclimatised to all the caprices of a Mediterranean winter or—far more likely—was my own temperament not already like its weather? The sun here would ripen the grapes in January, if a breath of wind or a patch of icy shade were not enough to wither everything. Max, lying in your arms was like lying in a tomb made to my measurements and yet I rose up from that tomb and fled!

All that does not mean that I need stay on any longer with "those people". The only bond between us is idleness. Last year, May had another lover, less attractive and more considerate than this one. This one I accepted rather coldly and with a touch of embarrassment, whereas May flung herself into this new liaison with all the ardour and organising zeal that usually go into furnishing a new house.

May? I could do without her as well as without Jean. In a year, our intimacy has made no progress. We have discussed love, hygiene, dresses, hats, beauty creams and cooking without acquiring any more affection and esteem for each other. A dozen times I have left May, with no regrets: a dozen times she has gone off with no more affectionate goodbye than a handshake. And a dozen times chance has brought her back to me, turning up unexpectedly to wreck all my plans for an orderly life, my resolutions to settle down into wise, sober middle-age; turning up with the invariable exclamation: "I *am* a character, aren't I?" The moment she appears, the open book shuts of its own accord, the flow of thought and imagination dries up, the mind that was trying to soar is brought rudely back to earth. Even words themselves take flight; all that remain are two or three hundred everyday terms, some of them slangy, with which one can ask one's way, demand food and drink and make love, terms such as you find in a phrase-book for foreigners. And I don't assert my independence. I close the book, and I put on a dress to go off with May and Jean to some commonplace *boîte*.

I am perfectly well aware that May has not a will that overcomes mine, but an inner mechanism superior to my own, a whirling driving-power that is never slowed down by thoughts. She has taught me that one can dine without being hungry, talk without saying anything, laugh from sheer force of habit, drink out of human respect and live with a man in a state of complete servility while maintaining all the appearances of frantic independence. She is no stranger to bouts of neurasthenia and black depression but she knows two great physicians of the soul: the manicurist and the hairdresser. Should they fail, there is only the higher resort of opium and cocaine. If May, looking pale and heavy-eyed, drags herself from chair to chair, yawns, shivers, bursts into tears at a word and tries vainly not to think about her empty past and her empty future, she exclaims fervently: "Tell the manicurist to come up!" or "I'm going to have my hair washed". Then, reassured and relaxed, she abandons her stubby little paws or her golden hair to clever hands that know how to knead, how to scratch delicately, how to brush and polish and wave. Under their soothing, healing magic passes, May smiles, lends her ears to gossip and vague, flattering words and drifts off into the light doze of convalescence.

Is she gay? Men assure me that she is, but personally I do not find her so. Nature has drawn all the features of laughter itself in her round childish face; a Cupid's bow mouth that tilts up at the corners like her mischievous eyes, a short little nose with quivering nostrils. But gaiety is not a perpetual fidgeting that betrays a lack of security, it is not chatter full of recriminations, nor is it a craving for everything that intoxicates. Gaiety, it seems to me, is something calmer, something healthier, something more serious.

Fundamentally, perhaps, Jean is gayer than May. One does not often hear him speak and he scowls as readily as he smiles, but I recognise in him the serenity of those who have a good digestion. And, whereas May, who goes crazy the moment they start quarrelling, looks about and reaches for a pair of scissors or a hatpin, Jean simply strikes her with the flat of his heavy hand, not viciously but with a kind of athletic heartiness.

Decidedly, most decidedly, the time has come to leave these people! Whether I like it or not, they take up too much space, too much time in my life. True, my life is an empty waste, but every time May passes through it, she leaves a trodden-down goat-track where nothing will grow. Why linger on any longer? I go on and on repeating: "The fact is, I don't know these people", while every minute, this evening, is showing me them in a worse light—I know them too well.

Besides, I can guess what people must already be saying about our trio; a woman on her own, too intimate with a pair of dissipated lovers. Ah, how typical of me that is! The mere idea that I—nowadays an

obscure nonentity—might have been misjudged makes
me feel that Paris, the provinces, and various foreign
courts are all staring at me with an accusing eye. I
feel so hot with virtuous indignation that I am making
my bed warm. It was so cool just now with its sheets,
glossy from being ironed by cylindrical rollers; sheets
whose chaste smell of chlorine is not wholly disguised
by my perfume.

I had almost got to sleep, when someone in the
room next door returned and banged the door with
callous brutality. Then two shoes fell with a thud, probably hurled from one end of the room to the other and
so heavy that the man might have been wearing hob-
nailed clogs. Now he is walking about in his socks
but the warped floor-boards creak under the carpet
and I can tell when the traveller goes from the dressing-
table to the bedside table, from the bedside table into
the bathroom. In the bathroom that backs on to mine,
I can hear the clinking of the tooth-glass, the clatter-
ing fall of some silver or nickel object, the gush of
water splashing into the bath. Alas, I cannot avoid
being aware of the belated traveller's every movement and action. Steeling myself to weary resignation,
I wait for sleep to plunge him, at least for a few hours,
into oblivion. How I execrate that unknown guest, how
I wish Mr. X would be stricken by sudden paralysis,
even by death! I wait till he has finished prowling about,
emitting bellowing yawns, coughing, spitting, testing
his baritone voice with "Hmms" that make glassware
on my bedside table vibrate.

Above my head, the ceiling shudders under muffled
footsteps. The room on the other side of mine comes
to life with the sound of pit-a-patting and a shrill,
aggressive woman's voice. She is talking to someone
whose whispered replies I cannot hear; it sounds as if
she were having a quarrel over the telephone . . . I
wait. I set up an opposition to all these various noises
by remaining as rigidly still as a thief and hardly
breathing, as if to set an example of silence.

The bell in the corridor shrills twice, three times,

ten times under the pressure of a nervous finger; the lift stops with a reverberating "poum" that shakes the landing and the iron gate is violently slammed. A night typical of any hotel and in this life of mine, going from hotel to hotel, I have lost count of these ruined nights whose slow hours are registered by the dropping of boots, the banging of doors, coughing, and all the other clatter of the human stable. Now and then, above the sustained pedal bass of snores, my ear has caught violent overtones: the madman's revolver, the abominable scream of a hysterical woman and the choking nightmare of a gambler in Monte Carlo! The papiermâché partitions have often let me overhear softer moanings; the sighs and rustlings of tempestuous love making which I have rudely disturbed by a deliberate cough or a bang on the wall, for I have become severe towards other people's sexual pleasures.

Nothing obliges me to go on enduring the trivial round of petty tortures that hotel life imposes on me. Tomorrow, if I liked, I could take refuge from them in a peaceful villa or a comfortable flat in Paris, for the death of my sister-in-law Margot has left me with a private income. Twenty-five thousand francs a year, for a woman like me, is riches. But there it is; for some reason or other, I don't want to. When a dog has been kept a long time on a lead, it does not go prancing off the moment you undo the catch of its chain; it goes on walking at a measured pace, instinctively calculating the length of an imaginary shackle. I go on with my hotel life, and why not? Broken, fitful sleep, meals at odd hours, chicory coffee and blueish milk, all that is part and parcel of my lot.

Besides, since I have given up my profession, I have acquired the rather selfish, perverse taste of lying in bed in the mornings while others all about me are up and doing. I admit it is a pleasure to me, at that hour when the growing daylight is drawing blue streaks between the slats of the shutters, to hear a valet rapping harshly on neighbouring doors, to imagine the weary awakenings and disgusted yawns, the hurry, the rainy morning, the missed train. A perverse, revengeful joy

makes me stretch myself between my warm sheets and
I have just time to murmur drowsily: "It's *their* turn
now . . ." before drifting off into the shallow, almost
conscious sleep of broad daylight, lit up from within
by the strange planets of a succession of dreams and
from without by the light that forces its way through
my half-closed eyelids.

I know it is probably late, but the electric clock
only marks the time by an imperceptible click every
sixty seconds. May and Jean must have finished their
quarrel, perhaps even their reconciliation? Someone is
snoring next door, a majestic ample snore as he
breathes in, interrupted, as he breathes out, by a comic,
macabre little *cloc*. It is a variety of snoring not unknown to me; I prefer it to the progressive snore which
begins low, grows louder and reaches its climax in a
violent fit of coughing. No doubt, at this moment,
Masseau's big nose is reverberating with a hollow
din, unless the opium lamp is still alight, its short flame
flickering at moments as a drop of sizzling syrup falls
into it.

I shall not sleep, but I shall not get impatient. This
particular night will be no longer and no shorter than
any other similar night. A night always comes to an
end, something which most insomniacs do not sufficiently realise. I excuse them, because nearly all of
them are ill. *I* am not ill, I am simply accustomed to
not sleeping. I do not turn on the light and I do not
open a book; excellent methods both of banishing shy
sleep and withering the eyelids. I merely wait. They
are odious, all those people behind the walls and above
the ceiling, wallowing in repose like glutted barbarians;
they are odious, but . . . they are there. Who can say
whether, instead of wanting to fly from their presence,
it is precisely their presence I seek? I may well have
deceived myself the day when, by leaving my home
and renouncing every domestic comfort, I supposed I
was taking one more step towards solitude. Flanked
by as many odious guardians as there are walls to
a room, I keep repeating, as if to convince myself more
firmly that they are there: "They're odious". And, thus

surrounded, thus reassured, I wait the cool rise of dawn over the sea, the higher surge of the waves under the morning wind and that indistinct paleness that creeps slowly into the room till it reaches my bed, my forehead, and finally my eyes, which from then on will be closed and insensible.

❧[3]❧

THEY SAY IT IS DIFFICULT FOR A WOMAN TO REMAIN indifferent to the spectacle of a man in tears. I do not remember that Max's tears, the day he wept so ingenuously over my approaching departure, seemed to me particularly moving.

But I do think, for a woman, that the sight of another woman's suffering is often poignant. It tends to arouse the sharp, egotistical fear we call presentiment, for it is nearly always herself a woman sees reflected in another woman's misery. She can almost formulate her presentiment, like a temporarily sober man looking at a sprawling drunk: "That's how I may well be on Sunday".

May is unhappy. I would have gladly dispensed with knowing this but a "real character", a "child of nature" prides herself on her frankness and regards the pouring out of the most embarrassing confidences as simple honesty.

Poor "real character"! There she was, in the room she had insisted on having to herself. There she was, miserable, among a gay, colourful disorder of silk chemises, open-work stockings, dresses with pointed trains or abbreviated skirts. Trunk-trays were strewn on the bed, a hat-box gaped open and May's chambermaid, a mulish Basque girl, was bustling about, looking sullen and disapproving. I also perceived, beside the tea-tray, two boxes of pills and a stubby little bottle full of white powder. May was yawning and sniffing; her nose was stopped up by the cold morning gloom with

29

flying clouds, by tears and, above all, by having taken cocaine.

"Blow your nose, May."

"What, and make my nose red! I'd much rather sniff!"

She laughed hoarsely, like a child who has screamed too much, for her grief—and I commend her for it—had not gushed out in lamentations. She had merely said: "There. That's that. It had to happen," then swore like a trooper and called Jean the vilest names. She had brought away with her, rolled up in her fist, a photograph of Jean on a postcard and a handful of banknotes, pilfered from her lover's waistcoat under cover of the general confusion. I would much have preferred to go up to my room again. My legs were bare under my dressing-gown and I was shivering from not having dried myself properly after my bath. I felt I was lacking in pity, in warmth—in other words, in affection—and I forced myself to be hearty.

"Now, now, May . . . it isn't serious, all this. Anyway, it's not the first time, is it?"

"The first time what? That I have taken a separate room? Goodness me, if I had as many thousand francs a year as Jean and me have had quarrels! I know perfectly well it isn't serious."

Nevertheless, she was settling herself in as if it were serious. She dragged the new dressing-table over to the window, tilted the mirror and began to do her face, a performance she will go through shamelessly in front of Jean, of myself, of the waiter or the little page-boy. She made a thorough job of it. There was a supplementary scouring of the ears and the corners of the mouth; even the eyelids were raised and turned up with the tip of a finger, as one does to the gills of a dubiously fresh fish.

Then May thrust her forefinger, wrapped in the corner of a handkerchief, into either nostril and cleaned them both out as vigorously as a rinser washing out tall champagne glasses. She scraped her tongue with an ivory spatula, cruelly squeezed out a minute blackhead between two nails, then set to work with the tweezers, plucking out hairs here and there.

"I've learnt by experience it isn't serious. But, after all, I know men, and, above all, I know Jean and I live with him. What did you say?"

I had said nothing. I had only turned away to hide the smile that was neither malicious nor kindly at hearing May say: "I know men". Why do women always utter this classic phrase not after a triumph but after a mortifying failure which would seem to prove just the contrary? I had said nothing, I do *not* know men.

"I've been living with him for a year," May went on, "and I can say without blowing my own trumpet he's not the sort that usually sticks to one woman for long."

With her hair scraped back like a Chinese woman's under a scarf twisted round her head, May was smoothing a liberal amount of cold cream into her cheeks and her forehead. However, she was so desperately anxious to convince me that she interrupted her massage and continued her speech, gesticulating with all her fingers outspread. I thought of the old days of putting on and removing make-up; I thought of the time when Brague used to call me, when my face was all shiny with vaseline, "the rat that tumbled into the oil".

"A year with a man: that begins to look like a permanent set-up, even though we've only actually lived together at the sea-side or in water places. Sharing a flat together . . . no, that wouldn't suit us. He's got his affairs to see to and I've got my own ideas. There are things I just won't accept. What did you say?"

I had said nothing. But May's fine instinct warned her each time she came up against my incredulity. Things she just won't accept? What things? She takes money, accepts blows, swallows insults—all, it is true, with the imperious air of a little tyrant.

"The fact is, if Jean stops with me . . . oh, don't worry, I'm not getting myself into a state! Perhaps it's more out of vanity than because he's fond of me, because he knows *I'm* a character too, in my own way, and not an easy-going one either. I can be led, but I can't and won't be driven. There's the proof of it!" May wound up proudly, pointing to her open trunks.

"I said to him: 'Au revoir, my boy, in this world or the next'. There!"

She was lying. Her bluff was touching, poor little May. At least it *ought* to have been touching. A man would have been sorry for her, or even a woman—any other than myself.

For she was talking about this lover whom she boasted of having said goodbye to and whom she reckoned to see again tonight, tomorrow, almost at once, as if she had just lost him for ever. She was running him down and remembering him and regretting him as if he was already part of her past.

I did what I could for May, that is to say I listened to her and nodded from time to time. By now her face was powdered mauve and touched with bright pink under the eyes that she had accentuated with grey eyeshadow to make them look voluptuously heavy. Eyelashes . . . mouth . . . a big velvet beauty-spot at the corner of her mouth. It was finished.

She smiled at me absent-mindedly in the glass and said, "How you're staring at me, Renée! You make me think of Jean when he says: 'What an ugly sight a pretty woman's toilet is!' He can be very difficult sometimes, the filthy brute!"

"Then why do you do all this redecorating in front of him?"

Her charming eyes opened wide with surprise between the stiff hedges of eyelashes.

"My dear! I don't say that when I'm thirty-five or forty, I won't hide when I do up my face, but now! I haven't got pimples, have I? Or wrinkles, or red-rimmed eyes? Nothing to hide, anyone can have a good look at it! Either one's natural, or one isn't. Shh!"

"What is it?"

"I thought I could hear his footsteps."

She listened. But he did not come.

"Tell me, May, has there been something more serious than usual between you?"

She looked at me; perplexed and, this time, sincere.

"Why . . . no . . . that's just it. On the contrary. That staggers me a little. You could almost say that practically nothing's happened. We didn't have a fight.

I haven't got any marks. It's funny. For some days he's been nasty underneath. He's been putting on his dreamy, far away look—you know, what I call his gigolo's face."

She chewed the bright red lipstick on her lips and stared out over the sea, that was shadowed with grey and a bilious green, with a gaze in which I thought I could read the astonishment and incomprehension of a creature unjustly threatened. And suddenly I saw again, very clearly, Jean's half-masked face; the mouth with the deeply-incised corners, the faun-like cheekbones, the chin cleft with a dimple and the robust neck, padded with soft flesh. Suddenly I saw again that mysterious eyeless visage, and I was sorry for little May, for that man's face revealed all the characteristics of guile, of slightly brutal power and of a weakness attractive enough to obtain all he wanted. In other words, there was no doubt that he was the *stronger*.

"May we come in?"
"Who is 'we'?"
"Us!"

It was a reedy voice which I did not recognise as May's pretty mezzo-soprano; she has a tone of voice that lends charm to her speech. I opened the door and found myself face to face with two men. The one who was speaking in falsetto was Masseau. Either he had got up early or he had not gone to bed at all, for Jean had met him taking a walk on the beach, looking, as usual, like a bilious judge. He was wearing grey kid gloves, a soft felt hat, a perfectly ordinary tie, yet, for some reason, worn by him they took on an air of extravagant oddity. Moreover he had just walked along the Promenade and through the vestibule of the hotel decked in a wrinkled strand of seaweed, as broad as two fists, which he had found down by the sea and pinned round his neck. Going over to the looking-glass on my dressing-table, he arranged this piece of marine frippery in the form of a ruff and murmured, as if to himself, "Columbine!"

"Masseau, are you mad? Take that thing off, you smell of raw mussels."

"One of two things," said Masseau. "Either you are the slave of a prejudice known as 'Fashion' and I spurn you. Or else, in the depths of your heart, you are offering me what every woman radiates at the sight of me: love. In which case, you adore my caprice, the whim of a gladsome morn. Or else again . . . But I should have said: 'One of *three* things.' I shall begin all over again. One of three things . . ."

"Jean, can't you take that object off him?"

"Good heavens, no. I don't know what he's done to me but I'm powerless against Masseau. If we lived on the other side of the world, I'd be a king and I'd set Masseau up as a holy man, stark naked under a baobab."

"I've been one," said Masseau coldly. "One soon gets tired of it, and the health of a holy man on the other side of the world is bound to be deplorable. Innumerable offerings of the faithful, fruit, rice with saffron, mutton with rice, rice with sugar: it's the dilatation of the stomach that ruins the profession."

Normally I am terrified of mad people, but, like Jean, I feel the attraction of this monomaniac. It is impossible to know, with Masseau, where pretence begins. He confided to me once that he is far enough gone to *see,* written in front of him, the sentence he is uttering and he cannot restrain himself from making little dabs in the air to mark its punctuation. When at moments he recovers, as he did just then, a rapid, clipped speech, with no grammatical redundancies, it is always for brief anecdotes, shorn of all verisimilitude, yet which I feel prepared to accept as authentic. May detests Masseau, for she can manage neither to allure him nor to pierce his shell. In his presence, she is like a dog confronted with an impregnable hedgehog.

"Is May coming on after you, Jean, or are we picking her up on the way?"

"No to both questions," replied Jean, who was automatically correcting the alignment of my silver-backed brushes. "May's not feeling well, she isn't having lunch."

"Is she ill? I'll go and . . ."

He turned round sharply.

"It's very nice of you, but don't budge. She wants to sleep. All she's asked for is an egg and some consommé."

He took not the slightest pains to make me believe him; he merely said what was necessary, without pressing the point. He looked as healthy as a dark man with a slightly greenish tinge to his skin can look, and, with his typical impertinence, he was taking the stoppers, one by one, out of my scent bottles. I did not press the point either.

"Right! We'll enquire after the child after lunch. Shall we go down? Masseau! Goodness, now he's busy with his correspondence! Masseau!"

"I'm all yours," said Masseau. "All yours and . . ." (he pointed to the letter he was writing) . . . "and Its."

I waited, irritated. I didn't like his using my writing table nor Jean's opening and sniffing my perfumes and my boxes of powder. I didn't very much like someone coming into my untidy, scented bedroom, nor someone indicating a loose strand of hair on my nape by brushing it with his finger, nor someone removing a thread clinging to my skirt, just a little above the knee. I have developed a physical intransigence which is justifiable, if not amiable, and I had considerable difficulty in hiding it under a forced good fellowship.

Luckily, it was fine. In this part of the world, fine weather makes up for everything and can take the place of a happy love life as well as a topic of conversation.

"Isn't it a lovely day? What a pity that May . . . They say it's snowing in Paris. . . . Where's Masseau?"

"Leaving his seaweed in the cloakroom. Hors d'œuvre?"

"No, not this morning. Isn't this heat incredible?"

Instinctively, I held up my face to a shaft of sunlight, as if to let it kiss me; then, instinctively too, I quickly withdrew it. "When I'm thirty-five or forty . . ." May had said. And, as she was saying it, I was staring at her uncovered forehead and temples and her clear-cut jawline. I lowered my head so that my hat should cast a little more shadow over my cheeks and I pulled

my hands a little further forward on the table-cloth,
my well-groomed hands that are no longer ruined by
wet-white or by wresting with trunk-straps.

"Nice diamond," observed Jean.

"You might at least have said: 'Nice hands', you
uncivil man!"

"I might indeed have said so, but anyone can pay
you a compliment on your hands, whereas there are
very few men who really appreciate good stones."

I laughed, and, as I did so, I released something:
though I had often found myself alone with May, without Jean, this was the first time that May's absence
had left Jean and myself alone together.

"Jean, before Masseau comes back, what's the matter
with May? Are you still furious with each other?
They're so absurd, all these dramas over a shaving-
brush or a button-hook! Honestly, you ought . . ."

On hearing me use the word "ought" to him, May's
lover assumed a peculiarly insolent attitude. He put his
hands in his pockets, flung back his head and whistled,
looking at me under his lashes. I blushed, having been
unaccustomed for years to a certain type of masculine
rudeness. May, however bitterly she might have regretted it later, would have slapped that "gigolo's face"
whose expression is nearly always more youthful than
its features.

"I beg your pardon. I'm meddling in something that
doesn't concern me."

"For one thing. And for another," he added, sitting
upright again, "what does it matter to you?"

"What do you mean, what does it matter to me? You
tell me that May's ill, I saw her yesterday morning—
ah, here comes Masseau!—I saw her all to pieces in
the middle of moving her things, so . . ."

"Ah, of course, so it's out of friendliness? Masseau,
we haven't ordered anything for you. *Entrecôte béar-
naise* do you?"

"It appeals to me passionately."

"Good! So it's out of friendliness, my dear Renée
Néré, that you're making this attempt at reconciliation?"

I liked nothing about that particular moment, neither

our table which seemed too big in the absence of May,
nor this argument in which I did not want to be involved, nor Jean's manner. Having dealt so abruptly
with Masseau, he was now talking with the precision
and the affected restraint of a man in a rage.

"So it was out of friendship? Friendship for May
rather than myself, I presume. But you haven't any
genuine friendship for May, have you?"

"That's an idiotic question!"

It was easier to lose my temper than to lie. I could
not make out what he was driving at; was he hoping
to induce me to speak ill of his mistress? My appetite
deserted me. All at once I had a distressing sensation
of being divorced from reality. Everything receded far
away and became very small, distinct and dissociated
from me; the place where I was, the people eating at
other tables, the treacherous sunlight and the man sitting opposite me, his bright eyes, of a mutable grey,
fixed on mine.

"It's idiotic, and insulting. Yes, insulting—both to
her and to me. There's no need to laugh. Masseau, I
appeal to you."

But all I could see of Masseau, who had taken refuge
behind a newspaper, was a bony hand raised to dis-
claim all responsibility. I weakened, and, like a coward,
asked Jean, "Why did you say such a thing to me?"

"To amuse myself, and also because it's what I think.
Come now, May's a nice little thing, but a woman like
you . . ."

His unfinished sentence contained exactly what was
most calculated to arouse my distrust; a compliment to
myself and the worst possible insult to his mistress. He
had already called her, in front of me, "an unattractive
little tart" and even "a poseuse", but to go as far as
accusing her, with false commiseration, of being "a nice
little thing"! Masseau reappeared from behind his
paper, blinking satanically, as if he hoped for some
more unforgivable words.

"What do you mean—a woman like me? To begin
with, I'm not in the least a woman-like-me. I'm a
creature who adores the good things of this world and
who likes soufflé potatoes when they're hot."

Masseau had taken a fountain-pen out of his pocket and was inscribing on his soufflé potatoes—they were as big and round as beach-pebbles—*Souvenir of Tréport; Biarritz, Queen of Resorts; Dieppe, Summer 1912.* Then he arranged them round the rim of his plate, but ate nothing. When he was handed the dish of steak, he gasped "What is this dead animal?" in such a horrified tone that I refused my almost raw meat, to the immense delight of Jean, who burst out laughing. He laughs, not like a light-hearted man but like a rather malicious child.

"It must ruin anyone's temper to live with you, Jean! You never laugh except at catastrophes. No! I definitely *don't* want this meat. Order me all sorts of cheese, a pot of cream and some fruit. As for you, Masseau, I hope your worthy companion burns all the pipes she cooks for you tonight. Anyway, are we going to go on sitting here for ever? We seem to be taking an interminable time over lunch today!"

Jean began to think of the afternoon that lay ahead, of May waiting for him, and became gloomy. The excellent coffee, with cream on it, along with our cigarettes, brought all three of us back to a state of euphoria, all the more precious and perfect for being fleeting. My nostrils were filled only with the pleasant aromas of peeled oranges, scalding coffee and fine tobacco. Jean was smoking with epicurean pleasure, and looking thoroughly cheerful again. He has a sensitive, impenetrable face, in which everything registers, but only in black and white, without tell-tale transitions.

The cropped head of one of the Impérial's little page-boys, knee-high to a gnat, suddenly appeared level with the top of the table and announced to Jean: "A letter for you, Sir. The lady said I was to give it you as soon as she'd gone."

"Gone?"

Jean gave us both a brusque, interrogating look before he opened the letter. He merely glanced at it, then thrust it under our noses. It was a pencilled note.

"Enjoy your lunch. I'm off. Goodbye.
May."

"What does this mean, Jean?"

The little page, who had not been running, pretended to be out of breath in his zeal to deliver the message and blinked his white rabbit's eyes. Jean shot a "Right, you needn't wait" forceful enough to knock him down and the white rabbit scuttled away.

"But, Jean, this is impossible! Suppose I go and ask at the desk?"

"Ask what? My dear woman, I implore you sit down and take off that expression of a lady who has lost her Belgian griffon. Your coffee will get cold."

He shifted back a little from the table, crossed his legs, and resumed his cigarette. But his nostrils were quivering and I could count his quickened heartbeats by the little jerks of his raised foot. We were almost alone in the dining-room and I would gladly have obeyed the secret wish of the waiters who were clearing the neighbouring tables and laying them for afternoon tea. Stealthily, I studied Jean's face, searching for the painful, heroic grimace that must have distorted Max's when, nearly three years ago now, he read my farewell letter: *"My darling Max, I'm going away . . ."* But all I could catch on Jean's features was an ambiguous expression of fluttering expectation, of indecision, an air of listening rather than brooding. And this gave him a new, tender face, averted from us and gazing out at the sea; a beautiful, lover's face brimming over not with tears but with hope.

"Masseau?"

Although I had spoken very low, nodding in the direction of the exit, Jean noticed it.

"You're not going? Why? Out of discretion? You . . . respect my grief? I don't demand so much from either of you, especially from you, Renée."

"Is that a dismissal, Sir?" said Masseau, theatrically flinging an imaginary *capa* over his shoulder.

"Of course not, old man, of course not. We're not going to make a tragic scene, just because poor little May . . ."

"Ah! Jean, don't start speaking ill of her again!"

I laughed, perfectly aware that I was not saying what I ought to say and that my slightest word was justifying what Jean had affirmed just now: "You are not May's friend."

"Heavens, no!" he sighed through the smoke. "At heart, there wasn't a better little creature living than that child."

Relieved, I pounced on the opening he offered me.

"Wasn't she? Wasn't she? . . . a thoroughly good little creature . . . with tremendous simplicity under her sophisticated air of 'knowing life' as she used to say. Isn't that true, Masseau? When you teased her, she used to go scarlet with rage, she took you dead seriously, like a child."

"Oh, certainly, certainly!" agreed Masseau with dangerous effusiveness. "Even if we were not always of the same opinion, she confided some delightful ideas of her own to me notably on foreign politics. On so many other things too, in particular on the rôle of religious feeling in modern music."

He rubbed his dry hands together, malicious as an old woman.

"That sort of joke's completely out of date, Masseau! At this moment, you look exactly like an aged fox contemplating a beautiful white grape. And that other one there, laughing! Oh! these men! Twenty-five, golden hair, flawless teeth, lovely eyes! All that's flung into their arms, and still they're not satisfied! Good heavens, what *do* you want?"

"I'm asking *you*," said Jean, in an artificial voice.

"After all, she loved you, that child! And you yourself, Jean . . ."

I had to take immense pains to keep up my factitious anger which was meeting with no response.

"I can still hear her complaining about you the other day and I am sure she had plenty of grievances!"

"Three or four thousand francs a month's worth, to talk like her. No, no, I'm not being a cad, I'm only joking. Poor little May. And poor little abandoned me."

What was the deep thought that lay behind those grey eyes? Ever since the arrival of the letter, Jean had not let himself go in one single spontaneous gesture. There had been no tear welling up on his lashes, no bang of his fist that threatened to smash the crockery, no furious exclamation that reveals wounded love in the act of denying it.

"Jean, what are you going to do? She can't be impossible to find, this child. Why, she's only just left. In two hours, in twelve at the most, you can catch her up."

"Me!"

There it was, at last, the spontaneous exclamation. But it was not the one I was expecting; it was an indignant bark, followed by a burst of outraged, angry laughter that made the glittering water dance in the carafes.

"Me, go after her? You think I'd do that when the thing . . . the thing . . . I can't find the right word . . . has happened to me . . . whatever it is that makes one want to say: 'It was decreed!' Go back, when I've barely begun to savour an amazing sense of . . . no, not liberty, it isn't that . . . yes, promise! I feel as if the mere fact of being on my own gives me the right to the whole world, and all the women in it. It's as if they were being promised to me, as if fate were on my side, and when I say *all women,* that means the one, the only one I want. Go after May when . . . when I'm here!"

A warm, strong hand pounced on mine, imprisoning it and enclosing it like a living shell. The gesture had been so sudden and the pressure so despotic that I was silent, as if he had struck me a violent blow. All I did was raise my eyes and stare stupidly at Jean, as he repeated in a lower voice: "Go after May!"

"You wouldn't have very far to go," said Masseau's old voice. "She's upstairs in her room. And it is at this point, my friends, I must ask you to excuse me. Senile student that I am . . . anaemic scion of a race which provided the world with Mister E. Man and all his ilk. I caused a line of poorly imitated handwriting to be transmitted to Jean. Now you know all."

He blinked, rubbed his dry fingers together till the joints cracked, and waited. He showed some courage, or else considerable insensibility, in waiting, for a rush of blood had darkened Jean's cheeks. My hand was still a prisoner and I felt as if I could not move as long as that hand was smothering mine. At last I felt free, and I heard Jean's slightly forced laugh.

"Incredibly funny! But why the hell did you do it, Masseau?"

"To see . . ." replied Masseau enigmatically.

Then his mania for buffoonery overcame him again. He put his table-napkin, that had been folded into a mitre, on his head, lowered his eyebrows, tightened his lips to make a thin, cruel mouth and announced himself, "Torquemada!"

[4]

THE ROOM IS OVER-HEATED, BUT THE OPEN WINDOW lets in a dampness that mists one's hair and moistens one's nostrils. After the stuffy train, after Nice, dry and blazing with premature sunshine, it is a delight, in this more northerly air, to breathe in the smell of rain no longer mixed with salt or iodine or with the enervating scent of mimosa. The wind wafts it to me across the grey Lake Leman, over which hang low clouds which part now and then to show a patch of clear sky against which Mont Blanc glitters, quite close.

I know this room, I recognise these pink walls set off by a lilac frieze, and the sky-blue doors. This is a decorous Swiss hotel, similar to innumerable other Swiss hotels along the lake and elsewhere. Paris did not appeal to me at all, and I remembered that Geneva, fanned by the wings of tame seagulls, is often mild at the end of February; I remembered too that Brague was giving his annual series of his repertoire there this week.

Twenty spots in the Midi might have tempted me, rather than Geneva; warm beaches between two red rocks, an Italian village, a little Provençal town fragrant with violets and jonquils. But I could not forget that these paradises, once the moment comes that deprives them of their only attraction, the sunshine, turn into sinister prisons. The tourist's evenings in them drag out interminably between the terrace and the out-of-tune piano, the reading-room haunted by ancient, bespectacled Anglo-Saxon ghosts, and the drawing-room, the refuge of young and old spinsters, reduced to a state of boredom that makes them want to scream and bite.

I am glad I came here. The chill sweetness of the air; the grey water, so smooth after the rain that the wake of a steamer stretches out behind it in a thin, narrow streak like a trailing rope: everything takes me far away from Nice, from May and from Jean. There is not a single thing here, down to the stiff, bare grace of a wintry bunch of barely budding chimonanthus branches, that does not rejuvenate me, that does not relieve me of the oppressive memory of my stay on the Riviera and of the scene that put an end to it.

I endured the company of the two lovers for another forty-eight hours. May, once again gay and amorous, had worn that overweening air of triumph that she assumes in public every time she knuckles under and humiliates herself in private. Jean, instead of adopting a moral attitude which would have set him up in my eyes, had taken the wise course of reverting to what he had been the day before and all the previous days.

It was on the eve of my departure that, having secretly packed my trunks, I consented to spend half the night in Masseau's bedroom-opium den, on the white mat and the chilly, smooth silk cushions. I myself do not smoke opium, but I allowed myself this night with those who do as a slightly shameful indulgence and also, as Masseau would say, "to see".

May flung herself ravenously on the opium, less anxious to savour the pleasure than to demonstrate her endurance. She talked of "the drug" and "the bamboo" and praised the syrupy opium with the competence of an old Chinese addict.

Jean set about smoking without conviction and without getting much out of it; he smoked hurriedly, as if anxious to arrive at the blessed moment when one lays one's drowsy, swimming head on the cushions. When he dropped his last pipe, he stretched out and gave a look aimed only at me, a look in which there was neither covetousness nor anxiety but a security as peaceful as death.

I was not lying so prone as the rest of them, and I

was separated from Jean by May, who was recumbent but fidgety, tortured by migraine and cramps in the stomach. I liked the muffled light of the red silk lantern and the silent busyness of the woman Masseau called his "congaï", a humble, ugly creature with beautiful, slave-like eyes. I could not really understand why those people, apart from Masseau, were smoking opium, but I forgave Jean when, overcome by it, he fell asleep like a man who has got drunk on purpose for the good of his health.

The short, almond-shaped flame in the glass bowl kept bringing my wandering gaze back to it and playing with the barely perceptible shadow of a rock-crystal Buddha that stood beside the lamp. Beyond Jean's body, Masseau's parched small hands, pale in the dusk, moved slowly to and fro, endowed with the precision, the intelligent carefulness that guides the hands of the blind.

Only one other painful hour, after that night; the one that preceded my leaving for the station. In front of an impassive Jean, I had to endure a hundred questions from a stupefied May.

"But why? But what's come over you? Jean, don't you think she's crazy? I bet ten louis that we'll see you back in these parts within a fortnight! There you see, it's the old urge to go 'on tour' coming over her again. At heart, she's every bit as much of a character as me!"

She addressed her remarks and exclamations, now to me, now to Jean and I was afraid she might compare our two faces, both of which looked equally determined to remain silent or to lie. Yet I had not exchanged a single word of connivance with her lover and he made no attempt to prevent my going.

My mind is at rest. I am delighted to have left those people in a civilised way, lightly without being involved either in a dramatic scene or a base flirtation. Chaste Switzerland is already imbuing me with a desire for a kind of retreat, a literary cure. Piled up in front of me, like slabs of solid nourishment, are the *Grande Revue,* the *Revue des Revues,* the *Revue de Paris,* the *Mercure de France,* and any number of less famous ones! I have enough to read, night and day, for the entire week! Already, before cutting their pages, I have extracted enough from them to despise the companions I have left, with the exception of the irresponsible, well-read, mysterious Masseau. I withdraw myself from them, thinking, with conceited amazement: However could I have lived three whole weeks with those people and made do with the five hundred unvarying words of their vocabulary?

Two hundred words to order food and drink; a hundred, plus a few numbers, to evaluate a passing dress and the woman inside it; a hundred to suffice for all the smutty stories; the final hundred for the subjects that "elevate the mind", art, literature and morality: they suffice for all that and more. Why, it was enough to make one forget one's mother tongue, living in that verbal desert! Brague's slang, the backstage pidgin-English of the music-halls, anything was preferable to the conversation of May and Jean which I had put up with, goodness knows why!

A shower, hurrying across the sky towards the two, has extinguished Mont Blanc which, up till then, was glittering with a harsh incandescence under a distant shaft of sunlight. Against the low, dark sky all the whirling seagulls have turned into snowflakes and, though I have just picked up a thick orange *Revue* from the pile, my thoughts take on a different hue.

Yes, I put up with those people. I put up with them out of cool arrogance, the inveterate arrogance of a former blue-stocking who could smile with ironic compassion at May's linguistic "bricks", at Jean's slipshodness, often too lazy to finish a sentence. Two days out of there, I went about with them only to indulge in the silent disdain of a poor schoolmistress for the idle rich. The third day, I probably justified their idea that I was exactly like them, a gay eating and drinking animal, conditioned to expensive meals, flower-decked tables and motor-cars, to the whole slightly meretricious surface of this life made for light women and wealthy men.

It is not enough to say I put up with those people, because I tried to charm them. For whom, if not for them, did I use such means as I have, a stock-in-trade which every passing year restricts or changes? The attractions I stressed were gaiety—the ready gaiety of women who are no longer very young and who laugh on the least provocation—and the conscious radiance of a serene temperament and a healthy appetite; those were the qualities that might humiliate May's agitated, unsure-of-itself, twenty-five. Twenty-five is not the age of serenity; adolescence is still too close—excitable adolescence, prone to suicide one moment, prone to extravagant hopes the next. A May of twenty-five wastes time in tears and dramatics, in little illnesses, in black depression. A Renée Néré of thirty-six demands nothing, and, merely by being herself, seems to offer everything.

I was not always unaware that, in the public eye, even my defects could stand me in good stead, for a woman is only beautiful by comparison. When I was seen in May's company, I cunningly affected a serene silence, a harmonious stillness, so that she should evoke the image of a half-ripe fruit hanging on a wind-tossed branch.

By so doing, I made use of an adroit defence, which did not pass unnoticed, for Jean's words are still ringing in my ears: "The fact is, you're not fond of May, are you?" Had I not merely deserved but invited them as a slightly stinging retribution for my malicious showing-off?

Thank heaven, I have left those people in time and with nothing to blame myself for except thoughtlessness in not considering Jean's feelings enough. I do not attribute much importance to his behaviour the other day. It is typical of many susceptible lovers, when their mistress leaves them, to exclaim to another woman: "*You're* the one I really wanted, how lucky this is!" What was imprudent was letting myself drift into practically living in common with Jean and May. It was inevitable that the normal, basic instinct of polygamy would be aroused in Jean by the habit and the demands of living between two women and that desire would eventually follow. . . . You are a man, you are the friend of a woman without a lover, you invite her out and seek her company because she is neither stupid nor heavy on the hand. When your mistress is bored, you rely on the friend to amuse her, and then, some night or other, when you stretch out two listless arms, the two arms close about the necks of both women and everything is spoilt—or everything settles into a new pattern.

I have settled everything in the best possible way. There are no broken bones anywhere and now I am perfectly free to . . . Perfectly free to do what? The wildest dissipation of Geneva are within my reach. Shall I go and throw bread to the tame seagulls? Shall I take a boat and have lunch at Nyon at that little inn where Brague and I indulged in tepid tea and raspberry wine?

There are also the cinemas. A positive orgy! as May would say. After that, it would be time to have dinner and then to cross a few bridges to go and see Brague at the *Eden* and enjoy his surprise.

Perhaps I would have taken the boat, but the seagulls detained me. At the first piece of bread, there are one, two, five then a hundred, before one has time to see where they appear from. They snatch it swarming, now swerving, now rising, now soaring; clever as trained pigeons, but with the fierce little heads of wild birds and wary, malicious eyes. They scream, fight, plummet head first on to the water at the same moment as the pieces of bread. One was always cheekier than the others and would hover at the level of my face, standing in the air and beating its wings, displaying the tempting whiteness of its belly and its feet with their outspread claws. I could have touched it, if it had been willing, merely by stretching out my arm, but it did not want to be touched. It stared at me with stern greed and never once let a piece of bread fall past its infallible beak.

Down below, on the transparent water, pierced by shafts of light now the sun had come out again, the heavy swans, white ones and black ones, rocked gently to and fro and gobbled up what the seagulls missed. Little black water-fowl, whose name I do not know, dived after fish with brilliant accuracy. The water was so clear that you could follow their plunging bodies

right to the bottom, heads arrow-straight, wings glued
to their indrawn sides, the delicate webbed feet closed
and inert.

Time slid by and I almost drifted off to sleep on the
bench of the landing-stage, dazed by the whirling of the
seagulls, the ripples on the water, the swaying of the
swans. I wanted nothing so much in the world as to
touch and clutch one of those living creatures, warm
under its feathers off which the water rolled in round
beads, to lay my finger on its impetuous little heart
and my lips on its smooth head. Or else I would have
liked to satisfy myself by painting them—if I could
paint—by modelling them—if I were a sculptor. Lacking hands that could mould and create, I sought vainly
for words to describe the reflection of blue water in the
hollow of a white wing; brand-new words to render
the richness and silkiness of plumage that defies waves
and showers.

Those sudden cravings to touch, those tender, nervous thrills aroused by contact with a smooth, soft
animal, I know very well what they are: the overflow
of the unused force of pent-up desire. I think no one
feels them so deeply as an old maid or a childless
woman.

"The Rat! The golden Rat!"
"The Celebrated Mime!"
"Give us a kiss, Rat!"
"Not on your life! Dry your paws first, and then
your snout. There! Now, I insist on being left in peace
till after the show."

I shrieked, I exaggerated my defensive gestures and
my disgusted grimaces to hide the fact that I was moved.
How could seeing him again, the man who had been
my stage-partner for six years, leave me cold? Seeing
him too in these familiar surroundings, in this seedy
cabin of a dressing-room with walls of bare boards!
The *Eden* is a former Circus which has long lost the
friendly reek of dung and warm litter. Given over now
to sporadic cinema shows, music-hall turns and light
comedies, none of its ephemeral managements has
taken the trouble to embellish it or to make it com-

fortable. Tonight, between two films, Brague is giving
Black Magic which is none other than our old *Capture*
remodelled, gingered up with "lascivious" dances, a
chaste imitation of a Black Mass, and a new set. Mademoiselle la Carmencita, my successor, displays her
curves in black on an orange poster, Renée Néré's own
posters, but the public does not examine them as
closely as all that. All the same, I could not help looking for my name in lights, over the porch of the *Eden,*
and I arrived in Brague's dressing-room feeling something of the jealousy of a betrayed mistress.

For nowadays he tours without me, this man who
was my gruff, honest friend; he tours with another
woman. Does he regret me? Was it the moisture of a
tear or the streak of violet grease-paint that made his
black eyes so brilliant? He would never tell me and our
first words were ironical, almost spiteful: he called me
Golden Rat because of Margot's legacy and I called
him Celebrated Mime in memory of a hand-out he had
written himself. But our genuine delight manifested
itself in laughter, in expressive noises that were once
ritual—the giggle of an English clown to which the
reply was the purr of an amorous tom-cat—in sparring
that revived my thrill of jealousy.

The dynamos rumbled under our feet and sent up
fumes of coal and oily iron as well as intolerable heat:
the place felt and smelt like a furnace. I undid my coat.

"Oho! The Rat's all dolled up like a lady," observed
Brague.

"I could hardly stroll about Nice, where I've just
come from, in the costume I wore in *The Capture,* old
boy."

"Why not? Splendid publicity!"

At heart, he disapproved of my get-up as "fancy
dress". He would have liked to see me in my regulation
uniform of the old days; a prim, severe tailormade of
the type only worn nowadays by governesses in austere
households and Royal Princesses.

I studied his appearance, too.

"Brague! Honestly, it isn't possible! You've still got
those same buckskin breeches in which you created
The Capture!"

"I shall die in them," announced Brague simply.

He was finishing his make-up with little touches of mysterious ingredients. I laughed with pleasure to see the same old litter on the shelf, the well-known litter of little brownish bottles, ochre-stained rags, paint-brushes. It bears not the slightest resemblance to a make-up box; you could swear Brague was preparing to varnish furniture or to do the brasses or even to polish his shoes.

"And . . . are things going well, Brague?"

"Not too bad, not too bad. I battle on, like the rest. It gets less and less easy."

"Oh!"

Facing me, ferocious from head to foot, from his black crêpe-hair moustache to his red leather mocca-sins, was the most fearsome Moldo-Walachian, wearing a Roumanian shirt, a Montenegrin belt in which glittered a long Greek pistol. In truth it was not difficult to believe this "Balkan Peril" when he asserted that he "battled on".

"Yes. You know, touring's coming to the end of its days. So I do odd jobs in cinemas, for a change. However, the main thing is I've started up a marvellous racket."

"Ah?"

"Yes. I'm teaching society women and girls deportment. Three or four Persian feasts and other *tableaux vivants* I've produced on the stage, and two or three mimes I've put on in the drawing-rooms of boot kings or tinned-vegetable princes were enough to launch me. These women want me."

"Ah?"

"You realise, every woman with b—— all to do in life has a mania to learn something totally useless and that costs a lot of money. Well, I teach them deportment! I've got a marvellous technique. To begin with, I get them together at eight in the morning till nine in the Cernuschi studio. The mere fact of getting out of bed so early makes them straight away imagine they're working. Once in the studio, I put myself at one end and then at the other and I shout at them: 'Come towards me, *walking naturally*'. You know the result. They start advancing as if they were on a tight-rope and quite likely fall flat on their faces in the process. It's an infallible way to start off."

"Really?"

"And even the ones who soon get discouraged or prefer to go off to another place to learn the tango—the frivolous ones, naturally—even those don't leave me without having learnt three indispensable things: to drape themselves in a scarf seven yards long—I don't provide the scarf; how to walk down a staircase without looking at their feet and how to hang garlands on the pedestal of a statue of Eros. If with all that, they're not armed for life!"

Brague was jubilant, overjoyed at being able to despise the "customer" who paid and had no understanding and to astonish the Rat, the Rat listening deferentially, sitting sideways on a wicker stool, like a lady paying a call.

"And . . . apart from that, are you pleased with the towns you're playing?"

"The towns are fine, it's the managements that aren't worth a button. Didn't I tell you about the business in Bordeaux?"

He came closer, his hand on the grip of his Greek pistol.

"Why, of course! You don't know about the Bordeaux affair! The third day we were there, the manager—and when I call him that, I'm being polite—decamps with the cash-box! You can see the picture: twenty-two poor devils out on the street, and the *diseuse* having hysterics and the woman-shot-from-a-cannon snivelling and all and sundry talking about going to the police and the Public Prosecutor, as if *they'd* ever been the slightest use! So what did I do? I called everyone together and I said to them . . ."

I listened, less attentively than I appeared to, but I listened all the same. I raised my eyebrows to signify astonishment, I nodded my head, and, though I slapped my thigh to show incredulity, I was convinced that the Bordeaux affair would be straightened out to the glory of the wise, astute Brague. And all during that time, I was thinking: "He hasn't asked *me* if things were going well. He hasn't asked me what I've been doing these last six months. That doesn't interest him because I've gone off on a path that isn't his, above all because I'm not working any more, because I'm finished. I don't exist any more, I'm no longer good for anything but pushing five francs through the box-office window if I want to see the show. Well, I'd better go off and do it!"

"Where are you dashing off to, Rat? That's only the bell for the interval you hear. We've still got a good ten minutes."

To force me to sit down again, Brague stretched out a hand covered with ochre grease-paint on which he had drawn, in blue pencil, gnarled veins and salient tendons that no one would see from the front of the house. This detail of useless conscientiousness softened my heart and I stayed, all the more because there was something I really wanted to know.

"Tell me, Brague, are you satisfied . . . I mean . . . are you satisfied with . . . my successor?"

He suddenly gave a beaming smile, or as beaming a one as his glued-on crêpe moustache permitted.

"Ah, that one!"

"What d'you mean, that one!"

"My dear Rat, you know I'm not easily staggered? Well, that girl does stagger me! She'd put it across to God the Father, she'd put it across to Senator Bérenger, if those two venerable personages frequented the halls. She's got something—I can't describe it—in her skin, in her eyes, in her hips. At the moment—you know the one—when I tear off her dress and raise the knife—at that moment, she bends her head back, thrusts the tip of her tongue between her teeth and makes eyes at the blade! It produces such an effect on the audience. I daren't say too much about it. I try to tell myself, among other clap-trap, that she has a special interpretation of the part . . . at bottom, I'm slightly ashamed of myself. Wait, I'll let you see the Object for yourself. Hi, you kid!"

He banged his fist against the board partition. A shrill voice from behind it replied "Yes", and the Object promptly made her entrance.

A very dark little person, whose Bordeaux origin sufficiently justified the Spanish name. She had thick, frizzy hair, eyes so brilliant that one would not venture to doubt they were expressive, flawless little teeth and a tongue reddened with liquid carmine. A plump behind and rather short in the leg; in fact, a sturdy little pony, with more mettle than breeding.

"Madame."

"Pleased to meet you, Madame. . . ."

"Brague tells me you're having a great success."

"Yes. I'm quite pleased. Obviously *The Capture* doesn't give me the same opportunities as creating a brand-new part. Still, I've tried to vary it, to adapt it to my style."

She fingered her hair in which she had stuck a pomegranate-flower and studied herself in the glass to avoid having to look at me. I felt her to be arrogant and extremely ill-disposed towards the "creatress" who had filched two hundred performances of *The Capture* from her. And I privately insulted her without opening my lips; I stared at her superciliously, soundlessly calling: "Dwarf, tobacco-jar, half-size siphon, white negress, cheap little miming tart." We were excessively prim and dignified with each other and gave a perfectly ridiculous display of conventional politenesses. I wanted to hit Brague, who went on stroking his stage moustache and looking as conceited as a cock over whom two hens were quarrelling.

"This time, it's our bell! Are you going in front, Rat dear? Shall I tell them to give you a seat?"

"Certainly not! I'm part of the 'swinish paying public' these days. I insist on producing my five francs!"

"Quite right, I keep forgetting she's made of money these days, this Rat! Hear that, kid? She wants to squash us with her five bob! All right, we'll let her have her way!"

I left them, laughing, and bitterly hurt. He had said "we" as if on purpose. To banish me in so many words from the kingdom that was once mine. Once the first warmth was over, he had been oblivious, complacent, egotistic. He had found not only a satisfactory understudy, but also, quite obviously, an easy-going, dissolute partner who gave him and demanded from him a trivial sexual pleasure. He had told me the story of Bordeaux and promised me the story of Brussels, but *my* "stories", of Nice and elsewhere, were not worth his enquiring about. Henceforth nothing would ever make me regain my lost prestige in the eyes of Brague. If I were to tell him: "I'm marrying a millionaire", or "I'm becoming a nun", he would reply: "That's your business; but just listen while I tell you about my affair with the leader of the claque at the Kursaal, in Lyons, you'll split your sides."

"Not through there, Madame! That door's only to be used by people working in the theatre. The staircase on the right, if you please."

I turned away meekly, with the submissiveness of an ordinary spectator, which is what I am now. Ah, they don't have to tell me to my face that I'm no longer anything in the theatre. A year ago I'd have answered that Genevan stage-manager back in rich Parisian language in which every word is an outrage to respectability. But I've quickly lost the particular insolence that is the hallmark of "the profession". A quite inoffensive insolence, really; a childish flouting of convention that is satisfied by such things as dining at a smart restaurant in a coat and skirt, reading the paper while eating and using a shy, over-familiar tone with the waiters. I no longer had the courage to assert myself. I obeyed the stage-manager's direction; I went down the staircase on the right which I knew as well as he did and eventually reached my five-franc stall. There I found myself wedged between two stout male neighbours who smelt of beer and tobacco. I could hear their heavy breathing and, do as I would, I could not help brushing against their knees and their arms. These prudish Genevans would have told me, had I asked them, what they thought of the "immorality of the stage".

When I came away, after *The Capture,* my heart was swollen with misery and jealousy. Anonymous among the crowd, I let myself be swept along towards the exit and out into the square that was glistening with rain, chewing the bitter cud of one of the last things my sister-in-law Margot had said to me: "You will lead a dignified life, and a dignified life for woman is one that leads her, unnoticed by almost everyone, to her grave."

Unnoticed! Poor Margot, she might well be gratified. Unnoticed. Was I ever more so than here, more so than tonight? Forgotten, dispossessed! There was no more place for me beside Brague and La Carmencita than between the two lovers back there in Nice.

If I were in Nice at this moment, I should have the bright lights of suppers at the *Bonne Hôtesse,* music that banishes thought, bubble-spangled wine, May's chatter and Masseau's lunacy. I should also have, to give value to every gesture, every glance, every word of mine, a man's desire, desire that would enrich me with everything I did not grant.

The best thing to do is to set off once more. What is the point of seeing Brague again here? Tonight's experience has been enough for me. My pride, both as a friend and as an actress, rebels too much, in the presence of Mademoiselle la Carmencita, at not being the leading lady in Brague's affections and the attraction on the posters: I do not want to become petty, spiteful, unjust. The brand-new railway time-table bought in Nice offers me its precious collaboration and my open window frames a patch of pure, rain-washed sky, above the black lake which mirrors drawn-out reflections of lights on the bridges and quays.

Set off again? . . . It is strange that, free and alone as I am, I give the impression of someone who is escaping, or being chased away. It seems as if there never is enough room for me in any place where there are people who embarrass me. Nice has become uninhabitable on account of May and Jean; Geneva cramps me because la Carmencita is playing here with Brague. I am ripe for a season in Paris and even a season of economy. A Golden Rat can live richly on two thousand francs a month, all the same she must not squander too much of it on railway fares.

I have almost run through my quarterly allowance and the only remedy for that is Paris. Paris, and not some corner of Normandy or Brittany, already green

under the spring rain; Paris, because I have neither the
energy nor the inclination to choose another refuge
and, most of all because . . . because . . . I will have
the courage to formulate a truth I have already known
for a year . . . because I do not know how to travel.

No. I really do *not* know how to travel. Years of
touring may have taught me how to pack a trunk, how
to read a time-table, how to get up between midnight
and six in the morning without shilly-shallying or
moaning, but all that was only the experience of any
commercial traveller. Even the craving for fresh landscapes and new cities only signifies in my case the freedom of the tramp or the restlessness of the homeless
who have no ties and who keep endlessly assuring
themselves: *"There,* I shall be better off than here;
there I shall find what I lack!" I no longer have the
right to doubt it.

Yet how ardently I longed for complete freedom in
the days when I walked round and round in a circle at
the end of a string! How I sang its praises, with the
lyricism of those who, living alone, re-write their own
lives in long monologues, in "effusions", admirable in
their way, but a trifle artificial.

I could safely lament, for I had foreseen everything,
except that the string would break.

The intoxication was, none the less, genuine, but it
did not last long; it was disturbed almost at once by
a strange kind of nostalgia for the treadmill which
expressed itself in sudden starts, in an obsessive need
to ask: "What time is it?" I still find it difficult not to
yield to this torture that afflicts the amputated, which
drives me to lunch earlier and more hurriedly on Sun-
days, to put my little Swiss watch beside my plate, well
in sight, when I am having dinner.

I went through some hateful weeks when every place
seemed to me tiresome and pointless because I no
longer had to find out, as soon as I arrived, which
street the beloved music-hall was in and the times of
rehearsals and performances. Frankly, it was during
that time, and not during my stage career, that I nearly
became exactly like Miss Herculea, the woman who
was shot from a cannon, who used to say in a gloomy

voice: "All these holes are the same. There's always a *house* where you're playing, a bad hotel where you sleep and a German brasserie where you blow yourself out with sauerkraut."

I struggled with myself, I scolded myself severely: "What, am I going to come to that too, to having no existence outside the theatre, am I going to come to that?" and that arrogant "I" meant "I, who am sensitive to the changing landscape, to the striped shawl passing by, to the crumbling, yet still solid red ruin; I, with my cultivated mind, my delicate perceptions."

Serenity returned; it always does. I had recourse to no one, except, mentally, to Maxime Dufferein-Chautel because I had to appeal to the man I regret more than anyone in the world and to Brague, Brague my friend, my scathing comforter, my thorny support. But the latter was gadding all over the place and fighting to make a living and the former had taken a wife, and it served me right.

Serenity always returns, on condition I buy it at a price. Each time I am the one who pays, or who gives in. A little walk round the town, then, the moment the intolerable staleness and uneasiness sets in, departure. It has become a habit, a hygienic measure I adopt without rhyme or reason. Jean and May quarrel, Masseau complicates the situation: I depart. Brague invites me to stay in Geneva, but Mademoiselle la Carmencita would derive only a mitigated pleasure from my staying and I myself am irritated by the presence of Mademoiselle la Carmencita: I am going to depart. It is very convenient, especially for the others, who never have to displace themselves.

Yes, I argue very sensibly about all these people and about myself, for it is not common sense that I lack. What I continue to lack is light-heartedness; I take everything seriously, as old maids do. The attentions of a Gentleman-on-his-own embarrass me, I make a tragedy out of Brague's indifference, and, on my oath, if one slightly sensual gesture to vent his spleen against May did not make me believe for a moment that Jean was about to offer me his life!

Three white swans are resting against the quay, not asleep, because I can make out the movement of their folding and unfolding necks and their treading the water disturbs the surface with frequent ripples. When do they sleep? This landscape of black water, garlanded with street-lamps, is pleasant to me because of all it contains of the already-seen, of the almost familiar. When I leave it, I shall go off to seek some other known setting, where the spire of a church, the silhouette of a mountain—not even as much as that; a noisy street, the welcoming face of a hotel proprietor who will call me by my name—will give me, for an hour, the illusion, not of arriving, but of *coming home*.

[5]

The HOTEL OMNIBUS DID NOT LEAVE FOR HALF-AN-
hour. Faithful to old rites of departure, I locked my
two trunks and packed my bag so as to give myself
the pleasure of having breakfast in peace, digging into
the pot of honey and the lump of butter with methodi-
cal greediness. The lake was the colour of a sick pearl,
even paler than the sky in which one could feel the sun
quite close, ready to burst through the clouds. A nice
morning for going away!

"Come in!"

It was my bill and a letter, a letter with the flap
hardly stuck down, that was not from Brague.

*"I am downstairs in the hall. I want to speak to you.
Can I come up?*

Jean."

"Just a moment! Waiter! Waiter! Can't you wait for
the answer? It's amazing, such shocking service! Tell
this gentleman . . . No, I'll come down. On second
thoughts, no. I'll give you a note to take. Stay outside
in the corridor a minute. I'll call you."

There was nothing to lose my head about, yet I felt
as if both my ears had been opened and a draught was
blowing right through my brain. I grabbed my gloves,
I put them back on the table, I flung the wet towels
trailing about on the carpet into the bathroom, then
I stared at myself in the glass, unable to put two simple
ideas together. During this moment of idiotic confusion,
I became aware of someone standing in the frame of

61

the open doorway, someone who was not Jean, but Masseau.

"Masseau! What on earth are you doing here?"

He had no overcoat on and was wearing his felt hat that was too small for him and grey kid gloves, ceremonial gloves without stitching and with overcast seams like a woman's gloves. Doffing his hat, he waited bareheaded, looking respectful and utterly fantastic.

"Whatever's going on now? For goodness sake come in. Is Jean downstairs?"

"No, Madame!"

"Oh! Well then?"

He came in, put down his hat and ungloved his delicate small yellow hands which he proceeded to rub together.

"He is not downstairs. For, had he been downstairs, he would already have been upstairs. And, if he were upstairs, I could not have replied to you, without jeopardising the truth: 'Yes, Madame, he is downstairs.' Now, one of two things . . ."

I cried out, exasperated: "No! No! Stop it. I haven't got time for fooling! Why are you here?"

"Why? Because I love you!"

"Idiot! Was it you again—writing that note? Does it amuse you, that sort of . . . mystification? (I'd like you to observe I'm using a polite word!) At least, one can't accuse you of varying your methods. They're very low, my poor friend!"

The poor friend, extremely calm, was eating the remains of my pot of honey and muttering, with a disgusted expression: "Three teaspoonfuls every two hours. Heavens, how nasty this medicine is!"

Then, having carefully wiped his moustache with my napkin, he deigned to reply: "My dear friend, one of two th . . ."

"Masseau! I shall smash a vase in a minute!"

"Either . . . I have committed a forgery in private correspondence, or I have not committed one. That is what we shall learn from the enquiry. But first it is incumbent upon us to know if: One, I have the right— Oh, boiling sap, oh hidden spring!—the—oh, lubricious awakening of an exacerbated male!—the right, I say, to be in love with you. Two, the right devolving on any thinking being of the masculine sex, Catholic and vaccinated, to bear the Christian name of Jean."

"What on earth do you mean?"

"My name is Jean," repeated Masseau in a flutting voice.

He had marked, in the air, the commas and dashes of his speech and seemed enchanted with himself. I sat down opposite him, feeling all at once very tired.

"Oh Lord, how exhausting life is with all you lot! How much truth is there in this story, and why are you here?"

"My name is Jean," repeated Masseau.

And, throwing back his head, narrowing his gaze between his lids, thrusting his chin out insolently, he achieved, for a couple of seconds—in spite of his goatee and his withered yellow skin—such a prodigious resemblance that I leapt up, roused by an inexplicable resentment.

"That is too stupid for words! Do you imagine I'm going to miss my train for the pleasure of admiring your portrait gallery? My dear Masseau, stop being horrid and tell me how you knew I was in Geneva? Lord, how stupid of me! I got the porter at the Impérial to get my ticket! So tell me, instead, *why* you came?"

I was using kindness and patience now, as one does with mad people. There must have been some cogent reason for that man to leave his white mats, his pipe and his lamp. But he was subtler than I was and I could not "pump" him so easily. He was not taken in by my cordiality and, besides he had seen me just now, through the open door.

"Be off, dear lady, be off! The anecdote is not really worth your missing your train. And yet Jean wanted . . ."

"What?"

"No, no, it's too late, be off!"

This sharp-nosed fox, this sham madman was pouncing on me, letting me go, then pouncing on me again, all in virtue of a name, the name of a man with whom, for the past four days, I ought to have been less obsessed.

"And look . . . here's the porter come to fetch your luggage."

"Tsst! Leave it there, will you? I shall take the . . . the two o'clock train."

"But, Madame, there isn't a two o'clock train," objected the bare-armed, red-faced lout.

"That's none of your business. I'll have a special put on!"

When the door was shut again, I slipped Masseau a humble, conniving smile; a discreditable smile that awaited the explanation. With one finger at the corner of his mouth, he gave a revolting smirk.

"I will tell all!" he cried. "But I want you to come and lunch with me at Ouchy."

"At Ouchy? Why at Ouchy rather than . . . all right, at Ouchy, I'm quite willing. But we've plenty of time; it's only nine o'clock. Between now and then . . ."

"Between now and then I want you to play bezique with me!"

"Bezique? Oh, cut it out!"

"I want to! I want to!" yapped Masseau, draped in my Indian bedspread. "Or the child I bear in my bosom will be born with a three-thousand-five-hundred on its nose."

He broke off his dramatic pacing to and fro and murmured, transfixed with admiration before the long glass of the wardrobe, "Oh! Eleanora Duse!"

Until it was time to catch the boat, I played six-pack bezique with the most cowardly complaisance and without extracting the faintest gleam of information from Masseau.

"Where are we lunching in Ouchy, Masseau?"

"At the Hôtel du Château, with Jean."

"With Jean?"

"My name is Jean," he said suavely. "Forty in knaves, without prejudice to a twenty in hearts I wouldn't discard for a medal blessed by the Pope."

I had stayed on and he was taking advantage of it. I stayed on as if Masseau were the devil in a morning-coat and as if, between our two fans of cards, lay a stake that we never mentioned. I stayed on, most of all,

because Masseau, with a madman's cunning, was helping to reawaken my dormant curiosity, my taste for
intrigue and adventure, the desire to be desired: there
is room for all these in my life and for things still
worse and still better. I was not unaware of this; but
the main thing was for them to turn up at the right
moment, like this providential buffoon.

Nevertheless I played faultlessly and I even won,
with my combinations of marriages and sequences; the
superficial complications of this game of a hundred
and ninety-two cards suited my present state of mind.
"A game for old caretakers," Brague called it. A game,
anyway, for women with nothing to do; with the bezique pack in the middle, a bag of chocolates to one's
right, a glass of liqueur to one's left, time passes.

"Masseau! What about May?"

Obviously, I might have put this question before the
boat left the quay. Anyway, Masseau was making his
farewells to the land and was not listening to me. He
was busy exchanging handkerchief-waves with a Swiss
family—grandmother, mother and four daughters—
who replied conscientiously to his signals. The boat
was crowded—it was Sunday—with proud young men
of the male-voice choir and girls of all ages, carrying
umbrellas and hold-alls embroidered in cross-stitch.

There was an abundance of "big girls", female children who had grown too fast and who were dressed
with an immodesty you do not see in France: short
dresses revealed women's legs, bare and downy above
ankle-socks; prematurely-developed breasts swelled out
childish brassières. They were embarrassing and in-
genuous, at once more innocent and more shameless
than French girls.

"How charming!" said Masseau. "Here at last we
have a nation that seems to understand and encourage
love in its two most convincing forms: rape and sadistic
murder! Wait a moment, I want to offer that sturdy
young person in the very inadequate skirt a collection
of postcards."

"Masseau, don't be disgusting! Masseau, I'm asking
you: what about May?"

His only reply was a glance, a spontaneous glance

that revealed the true Masseau, subtle and contemptuous. For the first time, I was conscious of feeling ashamed in his presence, as if in the presence of a man. Five minutes later, he was sitting between a girl of fifteen and her mother and chatting with them. With his hands crossed on the knob of his umbrella, he was imitating the sanctimonious expression, the furtive gaze and confidential mien of a bad priest and seemed to be no longer aware of my existence.

Drowsiness overcame me, the exquisite drowsiness of the open air; the drowsiness you feel on board ship, in a hammock or in an open car. The painted sides of the steamer, the sky and the far side of the lake were all the same muted greyish-white and the still air had the sweet, enervating smell of water with no salt in it.

Where was I going? I should know soon enough. At least I was being taken somewhere and for a few brief moments I recovered a peculiar sense of peace, the inert security of being simply a piece of luggage. I could feel the approach of an unknown will to which my own was already magnetised, like a sensitive needle. And since there was no question—at this moment—of fighting against it, I was aware only of its distant compulsion, its hypnotic charm.

How far would I have pursued that vague dream as I dozed with my eyes half-open, pleasantly conscious of the undulating line of misty green banks but not distracted by it? It was a shock to my optic nerves that awakened me; the sudden impingement on my sight of a massive obstacle, tall, square and capped with red tiles: the tower of the ancient castle of Ouchy.

"Say what you like, the Riviera is a gigantic sell! We've just had lunch out-of-doors, in Ouchy, at the end of February. How many times can one risk doing that before March or April in . . . well, anywhere in the entire Midi?"

I had not said "Nice", I had made a tiny little detour to avoid the word, like an ant going round a cinder, because I was thinking of that lunch at the Impérial, the one at which May was missing and I was aware that one of my companions was thinking of it too. Two

men all to myself as back there, and, now that we had
reached the coffee and brandy stage, the same odours,
all the more evident when the faint breeze dropped, of
the aftermath of a feast. How soon a good lunch begins
to smell nauseating!

A ray of pale sunlight made the sparkles of the
diamond I wear on my little finger dance on the table-
cloth in bright, tiny rainbows.

"Pretty hands," observed Jean, with a smile.

I looked at him reproachfully, shocked to realise
how closely his memories were following mine.

"Oh Jean, not really!"

I hoped he understood that far from being a coquettish protest, this was an attempt to head him off from
recalling and re-acting a recent scene.

Conversation languished, now that we were no longer
eating. Sitting at a table, stimulating themselves a little
with food and drink, is not that the only pleasure people who have nothing to say to each other can share?
Masseau was reading a Geneva newspaper and ap-
parently taking no notice of us, as if his mission were
accomplished. The delicately grey sky, the horizon
of dull silver mountains that bounded the lake made
a setting the colour of thawing snow against which our
three faces took on the yellow tinge of fever. I powdered my face and reddened my lips with the inefficient
aid of a pocket mirror, too small to be of much use.

"The left cheek," advised Jean. "It has as much right
to it as the other. Wipe your eyebrows. There!"

Secretly humiliated, I guessed that this morning he
did not find me pretty, that he was comparing me with
the Renée of Nice, and I nervously responded by "pull-
ing together" my tired features. Any woman instinctively performs this defiant feat of facial gymnastics—
which consists in faintly smiling to refine the shape of
the lips, raising the eyebrows, expanding the nostrils
and tightening the muscles under the slightly slacken-
ing chin—even for the uninterested eye of a passing
stranger. I had inopportunely forgotten it because I was
tormented by the desire to go to sleep and the need
to understand the situation. Had I dared, I would have
asked these two men, one of whom had just consti-

tuted himself the accomplice, almost the servant, of the other: "I implore you, tell me what is happening, or going to happen between us. Here we are in this bare garden, all three of us come from a very long distance, as if for a diplomatic conference or a conspiracy. A conspiracy against May? Then how is it I feel more involved and more menaced than the woman who is absent?"

But those were the things one could not say. Had Masseau been questioned, he would have disguised himself as Machiavelli and as to Jean, I know no one who inspires less confidence or with whom it would be more impossible to be frank and spontaneous. Moreover, at this moment, he was feeling resentful towards me. He had come by himself and, for four days, had been longing for the two of us to be alone together. For four days I had been constantly growing, in his mind, more beautiful, more mysterious, more seductive; for four days he had been incessantly cultivating his last image of me: a Renée Néré in a low-necked black dress who had pink cheeks and sparkling eyes. He had arrived to find a woman in travelling-clothes, a woman of thirty-six of whom people say "she definitely doesn't look her age", but mention the probable date of her birth.

His bright grey eyes scrutinised me impatiently as if they were searching for my vanished glory. In those eyes even love would not kindle the generous glow I remembered in Max's—Max who had cherished me all the more when I was ravaged by our rough games; my powder all rubbed off, my nose shiny, my cheeks marked with kisses and the traces of his teeth.

To greet our arrival, Jean had put on the charming, ingratiating smile of a man who hopes both to charm and to be forgiven and had promptly burst into a flood of gay chatter and explanations: May was returning to Paris but Jean had branched off at Lausanne to buy a boat, "look, here's a snapshot—pretty little craft, isn't she?" I had not found much to say, apart from one blundering remark: "So you're not angry with each other any more, you and May?"

"Angry? Why, I'd be a perfect brute if I were!

Angry with May? Poor kid, she's had enough of being dragged hither and thither, she's gone back to her little perch in Paris."

He brought all this out with unwonted frankness, with a kind of paternal solicitude for May, as if she were a convalescent. He kept deliberately bringing her name into every sentence, as if to make sure I understood the implication: "May is still there, we are doing nothing clandestine, let us innocently enjoy ourselves and above all, above all don't be afraid, don't withdraw into your shell!"

He soon dropped his manufactured exuberance. The great thing, now, was to reassure me! The attention he was focusing on me had not diminished but, as time went on, it had changed its character. Now it was tinged with a sternness to which it had no right; that is to say, not one that I ought to acknowledge.

I riposted as best I could. My gaze searched out and rested on every imperfection that marred this man's handsome face: the cheekbones that were too high and too broad for the delicate chin and gave him a slightly Mongolian look; the bull-like protuberance above the nose. Today, on the edge of the almost black hair, I could easily make out the blue of a narrow shaved margin, the trace of a discreet pruning back that daily heightened and ennobled brow! The rest I merely glanced at casually, avoiding the mouth, thick, but with sensitive corners, and the eyes, brighter than mine because moister. On account of the small, but round ears and the short lower teeth that looked as if they had been filed, I diagnosed: "Degeneracy!"—all the while envying this "degenerate" his beautiful pale nostrils, unspoilt by redness or blackheads, whose wings were welded to the face by a deep, well-chiselled groove. When he is silent, he has—I am exaggerating but I am not self-deceived—he has an air of distinction but he becomes commonplace when he talks and smiles. At that moment, I positively longed for him to make that mischievously gay grimace, to throw back his head and laugh in the way certain men pick up from living with loose women.

Brusquely, he snapped the catch of his cigarette-case

as if he meant to put an end to our mutual critical examination. I stood up to go. Jean rose too; my gesture had reawakened his dormant instinct of the chase.

"Where are you off to?"

"Why . . . I'm going back."

"Back where?"

"First to Geneva, then to Paris."

"Good idea. But . . . little motor drive first?"

"No thanks. The road by the lake is too boring for words."

"Little expedition in a sailing boat?"

"What boat? The one you're buying?"

"N . . . no. How about one of those charming little local craft making up that picture-postcard scene down there by the landing-stage?"

I hesitated, then accepted, but not because I particularly wanted to go for a sail. Ever since my arrival in Ouchy, my day had been spoilt by a sense of frustration, of having made a false start and put myself in a false position. Perhaps, if I made haste, there was still time to dissipate this uncomfortable feeling by some means or other. I no longer knew what I had come here for, but I knew very well that I had not had it; perhaps it needed only a moment, a word, a brief rest on the smooth water for me to go away calm and appeased.

The shore was receding but the sail still flapped feebly against the mast, slow to fill and heel over. Masseau, who had tried to make a sylph-like leap into the boat and fallen into two feet of water, had been left behind on the quay. He stood there, dripping like a wet umbrella and shouting nautical commands.

"Shorten sail! Mind the boom! Haul in the stern sheets! Let go the starboard anchor!"

We did not even laugh and our fresh-water sailor, who was handling the boat with the help of a small, barefooted boy, stared at the "madman" with an inscrutable, impassive politeness, like a good Swiss, accustomed to put up with the ways of tourists.

"Masseau will catch cold," I said, merely for the sake of saying something.

"Oh, it doesn't matter," replied Jean, absent-mindedly. His tone was apologetic, as if I had stepped on his foot.

"What do you mean, it doesn't matter? After all, that man isn't your servant!"

"That's why. If he were my servant, I'd be annoyed if he caught cold."

"What a sweet, kind nature you have!"

"Kind enough to lend a coat to a woman who hasn't enough on. Take this one, I can't bear to see you looking frozen."

It was true, I could feel myself turning pale, for the wind had brought the boat to life and it yielded to it with a screech of its taut canvas and a pleasant creaking of wood as it suddenly heeled over. I was cold and I buttoned myself into Jean's mackintosh coat; it smelt faintly of rubber, tobacco and a perfume that was not May's.

"I hope to goodness you're not feeling lake-sick?"

I laughed, my chin embedded in a turned-up collar that scratched like straw-matting.

"Good heavens, no! Only, you know, I had a very short night and ever since this morning I've had no chance to rest, so . . ."

"True, poor thing . . ."

He said no more, suddenly at a loss for words when it was a question of showing sympathy. I remembered a day when May was ill and he was looking after her. His face was indignant and he handled the cushions and the cups of hot drinks roughly, with a kind of enraged clumsiness. I never thought of that day till now and did not realise I had remembered it. The picture had just come up, clear and complete, in my mind, because Jean had said, "True, poor thing . . ."

"But you, Jean—aren't *you* going to freeze now?"

"I'm quite all right, thanks."

If I had exclaimed, in the typical manner of May: "Dear friend, don't you think the cold will play hell with your fatal beauty, braving the elements like that without your overcoat?" Jean would have replied in the same vein, and not with that curt, irritated "thanks". What had literally "cast a chill" over us was that sudden show of normal solicitude, simply expressed. Instead of that very natural gesture of masculine protectiveness bringing us closer, it made me want to call him "Sir".

The rudimentary accommodation of the boat—a small hard bench and soaked boards under our feet—increased our moral discomfort and reminded me of the days before I took to my wandering life. It brought back memories of moving house, of the misery of installing oneself in unfamiliar rooms, among furniture that has suddenly become unrecognisable. However hard I tried, I could not destroy that impression of some new and difficult *beginning*.

The water glided along either side of the boat in two slender, curling scrolls of very pale, very pure green, it felt almost warm to my cold hand.

"Why do all women trail their hands in the water when they are in a boat?" asked Jean.

I shrugged my shoulders.

"I don't know. I think all women make the same gestures at certain moments—confronted with a mirror, or a stretch of clear water—or passing by a flower or a very velvety fruit or material. They yield to their two invariable temptations. To adorn themselves—in other words, offering themselves. And to touch, which is the same as taking."

"All women—that makes a lot of women . . ."

"Not as many as you think."

"But more than you say, muse of false humility."

"Of false . . ."

"Yes, I mean it. I don't find it attractive, this way you have of treating women with contemptuous pity, as poor little creatures, not very complicated and not very interesting. And to make it convincing you add: 'I know something about them, since *I'm* like all the others. . . .' So, logically, the simple-minded listener concludes that you're not like any of them."

"But, Jean . . ."

"And when you generalise, as you've just been doing, it's neither from modesty nor conviction. It's just out of calculating laziness, to produce the maximum effect with the minimum of effort."

"But, Jean . . ."

"And when you answer me, if you do answer me, you'll restrict yourself to a few clever, facile words, but admirably supported by a look that means a hundred times more than what you say. For your trick—excuse the word—your particular personal trick is reticence, all the business of the lowered eyes, the secretive smile, the hand quickly withdrawn—in fact you convey everything in dumb-show, my dear, pure dumb-show! Lord, I'm hot! I knew I shouldn't need that overcoat. And now you can crush me with superior silence, but I shan't take back one word of what I've said."

"But, Jean, on the contrary! I'm listening, I'm amazed . . . I'm even impressed! It's not stupid at all, what you've just been saying!"

"And you can't conceal your amazement: 'Miraculous! He talks, he thinks! Joy, he's bullying me a little!'"

It was a singular spot for a conversation of this kind, our first, perhaps our only one. For he had just gone further in "generalising" than I authorised, by over-estimating my pleasure in being bullied. The wind had freshened and now our boat was swallowing the crests of the waves and a little sea slushed in the bottom, wetting the edge of my skirt. But Jean, excited, held up his cheeks to the fine spume and licked the tasteless water off his lips as it splashed us. The tower of Ouchy looked so tiny, back there on the land. I wanted to go back because I was feeling slightly ill; my back was tired and my head heavy, unlike this robust young man, swaggering in his unbuttoned jacket. But I dared not say so.

Illness is clement to very beautiful animals and very young human beings, the only creatures it does not disfigure. May used to admit, shamelessly: "My children, I'm tied up in knots with the gripes" or "I warn all present I want to vomit" and, in her state of physical collapse, she preserved a cynical grace that was not in the least repugnant; I can see the beautiful anguished eyes, ringed with black, and her green cheeks one rather too festive night.

I repeated feebly: "Miraculous! he speaks, he thinks. . . . Let's say, instead of 'miraculous', it's a surprise, and leave it at that."

Then I became mischievous again and I imitated Jean, the Jean of yesterday.

"'Snothing more than a wretched pub, 's Hôtel Paradenia!" "Forty horse-power's no use to me, I want a car with some speed." "Wine-waiter, have you any more of that Mouton-Rothschild you had last year?" "May, old girl, you're making a bloomer. That woman isn't thingummy's mistress, she's what's-his-name's late one, the one he used to call his old body—I recognise her necklace and the folds under her chin."

Jean's sensitive nostrils quivered slightly but his grey eyes, faintly green like the lake, began to smile.

"Well, why not? When I'm travelling, I try to speak the language of the country. Just as other people talk pidgin-English, *I* spend three quarters of the year talking pidgin-tart, pidgin-Jew, pidgin-playboy. But, all the same, I have a native language. And there are countries where I find it without having to look for it—yes, my dear, we'll go back, you had enough, eh?—charming countries where no one seems to know who I am, which put up their barriers at my approach, but which, at a word, I recognise as my own. Countries where I make my way, slowly—slowly you understand? as if I were going along a familiar path I'd allowed to become overgrown with briars."

[6]

When I was a child, I was very seldom taken to the theatre or to the circus. But on those nights the approach of evening found me in such a state of nerves that my hands were cold and I could not eat any dinner. The shock of the theatre lights, the first gust of music affected me so acutely that at first I could not look at anything; I was too busy keeping back the passionate tears I longed to shed and which I sensed would have been a delicious indulgence.

Just as my childhood has left me with unusual control over my tears, so I have also retained, with an intensity scarcely diminished by time, the ability to be moved by certain moments, and not only by those which irresistibly combine such things as the sound of a perfect orchestra, moonlight reflected on shining box-leaves and laurels and the smells of the earth when a summer storm is brooding. There are moments of idle weakness when brief, very old visual memories of contrasts of light and shadow are enough to melt some of the aridity of a heart that has deprived itself of loving. Thus the warm rosy glow of a lighted window in the side of a dark house, that oblong glow projected outside on to a sanded path or filtered through black foliage, has a special significance for me. It symbolises love, sheltered love, home, precious and lawful privacy.

When I leave the cold night outside and enter a bright, warm, welcoming room, it is not only my senses that are dazzled. I feel a compulsive inner excitement, a brief flutter of happy expectation, as if I were going to meet a lover. It does not last long, for I am never

75

expecting anyone; anyway, it has never lasted as long as it did tonight. The moment all three of us sat down at the table on the glaringly-lit veranda, such a wave of sheer joy went over me that I had to smile and clench my teeth to stop myself trembling. I thought I was utterly exhausted but I had no desire to rest. Moreover, it seemed to me that the state I was in depended entirely on myself and that the man sitting opposite me could have been removed and replaced by another without making the slightest difference. It seemed so, yet at the same time, I *knew* this was not true. I knew that my pallor, my tiredness, my slight aberrations of taste and touch—the iced champagne seemed to me tepid and the fork I was handling froze my fingers— had an obvious cause and were not accidental. They were the results or—to be frank—the victories of a silent, effective will which would weary perhaps, but which meanwhile was breaking me down.

I could not feel humiliated by this, since I was faced with such a strong adversary. The white shirt-front and dinner jacket set him off to advantage, with his smooth chin, his supple hair and those eyes, lighter than his skin, which make him look younger and give him an air of freshness and bloom. It was he who was dressed up tonight, for I had to keep on my travelling-suit, my wilted linen jabot and my toque with two little pointed wings. Masseau, drab and chilly, wrapped in unspoken thoughts, served as a second foil to him. I had to accept the fact that, though I was a woman dining with two men, I was not the high-light of the trio. It would have been so simple to go back to Geneva before dinner! But I had not wanted to.

Pleased that I had stayed, conscious of what it signified, Jean allowed himself to make coquettish gestures, a trifle suggestive of a tart displaying her charms. He smoked, with his elbow on the table and his little finger, which is slim and much shorter than his ring-finger, extended. He ran a finger between his collar and his Adam's apple, to draw attention to his neck which has stayed remarkably fresh, and, when he laughed, he deliberately prolonged his laugh in a canine grimace, with his lip curled up to show off his teeth.

Nevertheless, these little tricks, picked up from women, did not shock me. I came from a milieu where masculine and feminine beauty ranked equal, where you used the same appreciative words for the marvellous legs and narrow hips of a handsome gymnast as for the shapeliness of a female acrobat or dancer. Moreover, however little I had frequented "society" in my past life, I had had no difficulty in catching the men of that world using the same methods of attracting as the women and doing so every bit as obviously. So I let Jean parade in front of me like a circus horse, arching his chest, flashing his eyes and his teeth, and I refrained from checking him with a sarcastic word or a critical look. He was giving a performance for my benefit which I found anything but displeasing. And it was common honesty on his part that, neither at Nice nor this afternoon in the boat, had he mentioned the word "love" to me.

Honesty! Let us say a proof of good taste, or at least of tact. "I love you," Max had declared, in the very first hour. And, in his mouth, that great absolute word had seemed quite simple. He might have uttered it while eating, while blowing his nose, without provoking laughter or amazement. But Jean! I had only to imagine him murmuring the avowal to react at once with the incredulity of the offended surprise with which one greets a "bloomer". I had sometimes seen him behave like an ill-bred man, but never like a clumsy one.

The meal was soon over; we were the only diners in the almost empty hotel. The habit of being together, apart from the customary hours of eating and drinking, made us ask simultaneously: "What shall we do now?" And it was I who went on, without waiting, "Oh, Jean, there's only one thing for me to do, take the next train back to Geneva!"

"Go back? Again?" (His grey eyes hardened.) "This morning Masseau found you all set to go back to Paris. After lunch, you wanted to go back to Geneva; in the boat, you wanted to go back to the hotel. And now, this evening, you're starting it up all over again! Anyway, we'd better find out. Masseau, you haven't got a railway time-table on you?"

"I always have," said Masseau. "Lausanne . . . Lausanne. . . . Ah! here we are. Lausanne, 19.23, that's too late. Lausanne 21.7, which gets you to Geneva about midnight. Or else there's the still better train that leaves at 22 hours exactly and arrives at Geneva three-quarters-of-an-hour later."

"Three-quarters-of-an-hour later!!!"

Suspicious, I leaned over and observed that Masseau was "improvising" at sight for a little Ouest-État time-table.

"Masseau! Is that what you call a Swiss time-table?"

"It's quite good enough for you," said Masseau, unmoved. "For, one of two things . . . Ow! Either you are going back to Geneva or you are not going back. Therefore, you are not going back. This hotel's as good as the one in Geneva and . . . What? You haven't got even the most rudimentary luggage? Somewhere in a corner of my suitcase I have some delicate pink soap, stolen from a bathing establishment, which floats on the water."

"And I," said Jean eagerly, "have Indian silk nightshirts—white stripes on purple or green—and straw sandals."

"And I," said Masseau, going one better, "have a precious waistcoat knitted in maroon wool and a flannel belt unrivalled for keeping the lumbar regions warm. All this is yours, comma, if you will deign to accept it, full stop. You need add nothing to it but the contents of your 'little' handbag, yes, none other than that one, which could accommodate an entire roast lamb in its maw. And when one is such an experienced traveller as you are . . ."

I knew better than he that my handbag contained "all the necessaries". I am no longer twenty-five, to set out on a journey without my powder-puff! The debate did not last long; I gave in quickly, so as not to make my consent seem in any way important, and I asked Jean eagerly: "So what shall we do now, then? What shall we do?"

I caught sight of myself in the glass, fagged out, pale,

with hectic, painted red lips. I was afraid Jean might
feel sorry for me and advise me to go straight to bed.
No, no, I could not bring myself to finish this day like
that, I *would* not!

"Oh Jean, up there, in Lausanne, there's a music-
hall where I played two years ago, a ghastly beer-
soaked, smoky hole, where you can see films and pa-
thetically bad performing animals and twentieth-rate
singing-turns and . . ."

"Closed," interrupted Masseau. "Gone bankrupt."

"Did you get your information from the Ouest-État
time-table?" I asked acidly.

"No. The Ouest-État time-table is a well-composed
anthology, the fruit of a first-class mind, but, in some
respects, incomplete. I had to have recourse to the
hotel porter."

He addressed himself again to scribbling goodness
knows what in a little black notebook, his right shoulder hunched up in the classic pose of a quill-driver
deformed by long habit. One could see nothing but his
thin nose, pinched like a sick man's, and the top of his
bald head, sparsely striped by long plastered-down
hairs like flattened grass. Old devil that he was! Satan
disguised as a provincial notary, his cleft foot in a
square-toed shoe, and trafficking in haunted castles.
It seemed to me that his claw, clutching the fountain-
pen like a crab, wished me now good, now a little ill.

"Well, Jean, what shall we do, since . . ."

"Ssh!" interrupted Masseau.

"What is it now?"

Masseau raised a finger, unveiled his small eyes and
blinked in the direction of the garden.

"Rain."

I listened to the sudden shower that was beating on
the veranda and my resentment turned against Masseau.

"You did it on purpose!"

Jean's laugh made me think I had said something
funny, but I added sulkily, as if personally offended,
"Since that's that, I'm going to bed. Masseau, go and
ask for a room for me, that's the least you can do!" He
disappeared and I realised, too late, that I had spoken

to him more as if to a servant than to an obliging friend.

"I really might have done it myself. . . ."

"Don't worry," said Jean. "It amuses him."

They had just switched off half the lights on the veranda, an obvious hint that drove us into the hall, a covered-in courtyard of the old castle where ferns and stork's bill clung to the jointures of the stone walls. Against their massiveness the English furniture looked frail and flimsy.

I sat down at a little desk, and propped myself up on my elbows in a careless, provisional attitude. Jean half-seated himself on the arm of a chair. Obviously we were going to leave the hall in a moment, yet I did not even look as if I knew it was cold and deserted and that the miserly light was rebuking us for being still up at this hour. I stayed where I was, and Jean did not stir. And behind both our faces was the same fixed will: this interminable day, which for me had been harassing, spoilt by reticences and banalities, this empty, humiliating day—since my part in it was that of a woman who had come a long way to meet a man— had to be brought to a close by some word or some gesture that would ratify it or erase it. I had reached a point where I would have been content with very little. A false confidence would have sufficed me, one of those stories in which the anecdote is hardly more than a pretext for such remarks as "I don't know if you think as I do . . ." or "I've always been like that . . ." or "I only need to look at you to realise . . ."

But nothing came; neither word nor gesture. Nothing but nervous yawns and idiotic remarks about English taste in furniture.

I felt ashamed for him and of him, this man sitting side-saddle on the edge of an armchair, swinging one foot and staring at his patent leather shoe and the silken mesh of his sock.

I was ashamed of myself obviously *waiting* and I could feel the exasperating moment coming when this flagrant waiting would assume the force of a mute invitation, almost of deliberate provocation. I hated myself, and I hated Jean. Yet there I remained, stuck;

laughing and listening to myself talking. I gave a glance at Jean sitting there, a glance at the door through which Masseau should be returning any moment, a glance at the clock. Another five minutes, and I would go—yet another five minutes, but those would definitely be the last.

"That's just like me. I remember my husband once gave me some Dutch furniture. Like everyone else, I had 'the first Dutch furniture ever seen in Paris'; you get sick of it at once, that furniture without any style."

"When I furnish seriously, *I* shall allow that sort of fancy stuff in a smoking-room or a dressing-room."

"Or a kitchen."

"Yes, it could go in a kitchen too."

He had stood up; I felt it rather than saw it, for I was turning over the pages of a magazine. He was behind me; my whole back was watching him.

"A kitchen, now, one can do charming things with that. What always ruins a kitchen is the cook."

He had had his hands in his pockets; I had just heard him withdraw them.

"All the same, Jean, I remember, when I was staying in a very simple country house in England, admiring the delicious uniforms the servants wore—blue linen for the kitchen staff and pink linen . . ."

With his two free hands, Jean had seized me firmly by the elbows so that the nape of my neck understood at once what was wanted of it and bent forward—a movement to escape, if you like, but very convenient for choosing the place to kiss. A good kiss, warm, not too devouring; warm, long and tranquil; a kiss that took time to satisfy itself and that gave me, after the first shiver right down my spine, a slightly lethargic contentment. A good, static kiss, well given and well taken, which did not disturb the balanced poise of our two bodies, and to which I submitted, with eyes and mouth closed, with an inward sigh of relaxation: "Ah, how good I feel!"

". . . And pink linen for the housemaids."

"Charming," replied Jean, in a voice hardly lower. "A bit like a pink fondant, perhaps. Ah, there comes

our Masseau in person! Well, Masseau, have you got
her a room?"

Masseau rubbed his hands and stared at us between
the eyes as if he hoped for some remarkable revelation.
There was nothing to discover. We were very calm, just
as calm as before and I no longer looked bad-tempered.
Jean had his arms outstretched, but he might have been
yawning.

It might have been sleepiness too that made me so
hurriedly say goodnight to my two companions and
give them an absent smile as I proffered a warm, limp
hand.

What I have done is, I believe, what is known as putting one's head in the lion's mouth. All right. There I
am, there I stay. It is quite comfortable there and I
feel, at the moment, as calm as if I had already been
devoured. Jean? . . . Jean is on the floor below, in his
room. Or else, since it is no longer raining, he is taking
a walk by the lake. He is wherever he chooses to be.
It is as if he were less in my thoughts tonight than
he was this morning or these past few days.

With a sigh of exhaustion, I have just locked myself
into my room, which is at the top of the tower and all
windows. Gothic scrolls painted on the walls and the
ceiling would provide me with information about the
history of the ancient castle of Ouchy, but I am more
interested in the dressing-room and the steaming water
lashing into the bath.

The day that has just ended has drained all my ener-
gies and I resent these fifteen hours of moral tension,
anxiety and defensive coyness. Defensive? I might just
as well not have been! My inveterate romanticism had
been all prepared to be lyrical or scathing about Love.
As if this were a question of love! Let me take a deep
breath and consider—while my head is still just clear
enough not to let avidity muddle it—the thing I know
least about: the brief adventure. There are other names
for it, but I reject them because they are vile; the thing
itself is none too beautiful as it is! I can only congratu-
late myself in those feeble, slightly brutal phrases people use to a child who has burnt itself playing with

matches or come a cropper while running: "Well, are you satisfied now? Have you got what you wanted? Goodness knows you asked for it! Still, all's well that ends well!"

Someone was walking about, down below. It was Jean, or Masseau, or some other man. The thought that Jean might come up and knock at my door did not make me so much as raise my head. It was not insensibility, no, no, far from it! But what strange resignation! A kiss, and everything becomes simple and enjoyable and superficial—and also a trifle coarse. A kiss, and the soaring spirit comes down to earth like a cloud of summer midges beaten down by the first drops of a storm. For nothing could have been more explicit than that silent kiss. Not a tender word, not a whispered entreaty, not even the murmur of my name, nothing but that kiss given treacherously from behind and received with smug insincerity. I had barely interrupted a banal remark for it; I had neither hindered it or returned it. And how equally careful Jean had been to *forget* it so promptly afterwards! Our honest bodies have clung together with a mutual thrill of delight they will remember the next time they touch, while our souls will withdraw again behind the barrier of the same dishonest but expedient silence. Jean's signifies: "There's nothing to worry about; simply a question of pleasure, pleasure and still more pleasure. As to the rest, let's be careful to keep it out of it." And mine replies: "So there *is* a 'rest'? The idea hadn't even occurred to me. But don't worry, you're not the man who's likely to remind me of it."

Yet why should delicacy not play almost as great a part in our attitude as cynicism? I grant that Jean may want to safeguard my touchy independence as well as his own liberty; I may well concede him that, provided he understands what I am offering and what I am withholding: "You are reassuring me, but let me reassure you. Set your mind at rest. I do not intend to lean on you any more heavily, or any longer, in the future than I did just now in your arms. My weight is no more than the weight of a plant, momentarily broken down, and needing support only enough to revive and stand up-

right again." He will understand; if necessary I shall
have to tell him in so many words, if there is no other
way. We are not, I sincerely hope, going to indulge in
long bouts of "lovers' talk" or the mawkish confidences
of schoolgirls. It is our silence, the silence of higher
animals, that raises our hasty affair a little above the
commonplace. Let us remain silent. We should not, we
cannot talk of the past; the past is betrayed little May,
and other little Mays before her; it is my regretted, yet
dreaded, Max—solid, without a flaw or a crack in him
anywhere like a splendid, insuperable wall! We must
not talk of the future; to talk of the future is to talk of
love. Oh! let us go on being silent!

A great soothing calm pervades my whole body. It is
as if I had suddenly done with thinking. I feel as if I
had just arranged the minutest details of a project, all
the rites of a ceremony that must be performed soon,
and inevitably. I shall probably go right off to sleep
but I do not want to. What is the point of blind, total
sleep? If I do not close my rigid eyelids, tenuous pic-
tures flit across the dark blue screen of the windows.
These coloured projections are the comfort of my disturbed nights, the joy and entertainment of my calm
ones. Landscapes, known or invented, animated by
very few figures, illuminated by such varied lights shed
by such fabulous stars that their splendour or their
mysterious gloom make me proud of them, as if I were
painting them; that is all, that is enough.

I am about to fall fast asleep; real sleep and real
dreams, ordained, realistic, impervious dreams—*the
other life*—solicit me urgently. I resist, because I know
I am powerless to choose the scenery of that subter-
ranean kingdom and the sad figures that people it,
chosen from among the peaceful dead, friends long
vanished and forgotten children who played with me.
My recent friends and the casual acquaintances of my
present life do not descend into those depths. I resist
so as to remain with my frail apparitions of the upper
world, the ones I summon up on the blue screen of the
windows. Jean!

It is a faint summons, but it is answered. Here he is,
standing on a white terrace above a formal hotel gar-

den. Here he is, looking exactly like himself, but I have lost the key to his face and his gestures, which have become to me unintelligible. In his anonymous perfection, he is the Unknown Stranger. He follows me and disappears as soon as I turn round, but I am aware of his wish to be seen. I am walking along a path through a park, a path he has just trodden before; elder-flowers and pink spikes of tamarisk dangle, broken, at the level of my face, as if chewed by some tall straying animal.

I come to a circular clearing, floored with pale sand. Where can he hide himself here? There is no cover for him except these little low bushes, fragrant and black in the sunlight. But he hides himself in my shadow, like those devoted dogs who cling to their master's heels. He revolves with my shadow, insistently, almost abjectly, following my every movement to keep his shadow lying on mine.

I must keep walking! I am not fleeing but the inexorable unfolding of the dream drives me on. Unknown stranger, do you hear me? I am not fleeing. You would reckon my flight as a victory to you. I go further and further until I am in a bedroom which is mine, as all hotel bedrooms are mine, and into which you do not enter. Against the background of blue-grey sea that fills the space of the open window, I can see the bluer smoke of your cigarettes rising up like incense. If I were to lean out of the window, you would vanish again, leaving the air disturbingly redolent of smoke and of perfume. You have a sprig of heliotrope in your buttonhole. I cannot see it but I recognise its scent.

I must keep on walking! The dream, even if unconscious of time, is painfully aware of its own frailty and hurries on to a logical end which is at the mercy of a creaking board, the scrape of a rat's claw or a nervous jerk of the dreamer's body. I must walk on, so that I can feel you are tracking me, not like a swift, alert poacher, but with the sullen air of a half-wakened beast pursuing its prey out of lazy hunger. Ah! you are not giving yourself any trouble over me. Yet, all the same, you use one stratagem—beauty.

You are beautiful and I do not know who you are.

You were the one thing lacking in this torrid landscape and you had to appear. You complete the scenery of my dream, a necessary adjunct of it like the poplar standing up like a stiff plume on the hill, like the purple rock, like the green wave that suddenly bursts into white flame as it hurls itself on it. Do you demand more? It is enough, since you embody neither sorrow nor love, and moreover your face, your look, your irritating passivity reveal your true nature.

I do not know who you are and yet I insult you and I talk to you as if we were intimates. Now your shadow, unknown stranger, is growing larger beside mine on the path. You are going to overtake me; I can hear your long, lazy tread that makes a soft sound like the padding of heavy velvet paws. Overtake me, go ahead of me so that my eyes can wander down your shaven nape, all blue with black hairs, to your bare hands clenched and menacing. Let us go on walking, follow me, precede me, but do not speak. Why are you not dumb, beautiful ghost? Encompass me, surround me on all sides, let us hasten on together to the end of the dream, but do not speak to me.

Take advantage of this labyrinthine park, blazing with white sunshine and scarlet flowers, take advantage of this dull, inexorable music that comes from I know not where and drifts heavily on the breeze. Be content to remain, for a brief space neither you nor I can measure, a figure in a landscape.

I give you a tryst on this terrace beyond which there is nothing but the sea and the end of the dream. Come to that tryst slowly and in such silence that I may misjudge the distance between us, that you may come on me so suddenly and unawares that there is no room for me to stretch out my arm and thrust you away. Come, beautiful rock in my tranquil path; come that I may climb over you, since I do not want to avoid you.

{7}

"Yes, we're coming into Paris," said Jean.

He wiped the pane with a corner of the blind and tried to make out what was going on outside. The darkness showed him nothing but his own reflection and I could see his two faces, one light, one dark, forehead to forehead like two rams about to butt each other.

He stayed like that, glad perhaps to rest his weary gaze by fixing it on nothing but darkness. We had had enough of travelling sitting opposite each other.

With May, it had not been so tiring. I remembered a Jean fast asleep in the corner of a compartment, his head leaning sideways and his mouth half-open. I had pulled my veil down to my chin and retired from circulation while May, her right eye hidden by the peak of a leather cap, smoked twenty cigarettes, crumpled up newspapers and watched us with envy, wide-awake as a little owl. But today . . . To be honest, we had had some delightful interludes. It had been fun, for example, pretending to be a couple in the restaurant car, searching the list together for a wine that would console us for the Breton leg-of-mutton and saying to Jean under my breath with hypocritical reproach: "For goodness sake, don't look at me with that amiable expression! People will think we've just picked each other up in the corridor!"

We were alone in the compartment; I hardly counted the presence of the lady in pince-nez and of her little dog who refused to lie down, went to sleep standing up, toppled forward on its nose and woke itself and started all over again, just like Fossette, my deceased Fossette. I said to Jean: "If only you had known Fossette . . ." and I proceeded to quote some examples of canine intelligence. He received any brief anecdotes of my past with a polite, patient, faintly disgusted expression. All right, I'd be silent! Better still, I'd be angrily silent, passionately silent! On my side, I noticed that Jean put on a special expression when he spoke of his family or of himself.

He said: "My father . . . My uncle La Hourmette . . ." in a consciously flippant way, he said: "It was the year my poor good mother died," in a tone of kindly contempt and added, jestingly: "To a certain extent, we all make our mothers die of grief!"

I felt like retorting "*I* didn't", just to see his astonished expression: raised eyebrows and thrust-out chin. Do music-hall actresses *have* families? Good Lord, whatever can they be like? On the other hand, every allusion to May was greeted without the faintest embarrassment, even with enthusiasm. "We'll all three have lunch together this week, naturally."

I found *naturally* going rather too far and I replied with one of those "complicated" looks, into which Jean accuses me of putting too much. He applauded it, not without irony: "Excellent! Perhaps not absolutely an 'off-stage' look, but very good, all the same."

In a twelve-hour journey one can learn a good deal, even with very little talking. This contempt Jean did not hesitate to display for my former profession indicated that he thought about it enough to want to forget it and that he cared sufficiently to be preoccupied with something more than the desire of the coming night.

Twice he had abruptly got up as if he were going to stop the train and get out; then he had sat down again, very sedately.

"I apologise. Travelling in a train makes me bad-tempered. In a car, I'm delightful; but a train, this internment which . . ."

"Which goes on for ever . . ."

"Yes, exactly, which goes on for ever! We'd be better

anywhere than here. And, to begin with, your patience would exasperate a saint."

"I'm accustomed to trains, you know."

"Yes, I know, I know! Don't start the saga of your touring days again or I'll do something desperate!"

I laughed, because I was thinking of Max and because I already enjoy deceiving Jean about the causes of my mirth. I am certainly not acquiring a taste for virtue in his company.

Yet we were quite comfortable in this compartment that smelt of peeled oranges, dust and fresh newsprint. Only we had had enough of it. Our mutual attraction allowed us neither long silent rests nor long conversations nor prolonged disregard of it. Our sail had exhausted my patience, our meals together seemed to me interminable and he could not endure another second of this twelve hours' tête-à-tête. If he had dared, he would have exclaimed: "Let's play at something else."

Fickle passer-by, Unknown Stranger of my dream, I knew the game that would please you, and I was thinking of it too.

"It's easier," Jean had said. That is a word that covers much. Obviously it was easier for me to leave my baggage ticket with his manservant so that he could take my trunks to the Hôtel Meurice. To get into Jean's car and drive off at once over the greasy road surface was easier than waiting for a taxi. It is always easier to let oneself go than to restrain oneself.

Besides, nowadays, my trunks are merely my trunks and I entrust them to anyone. I no longer trail round that precious, shabby old object that contained our stage costumes, that treasure which gave Brague and myself such agonised qualms every time we arrived in a new town. "Look here, this infernal Railway Company has let the trunk go astray *again!*" Its tarred canvas displayed prominent wooden ribs, like a half-starved cab-horse; its corners, which we had had brass-bound at our common expense, defied the malevolence of theatrical wardrobe-men whose idea of "bringing down" a trunk is to give it one good shove at the top of the stairs as if they were chucking out some mug of a stage-door Johnny. Its sides, plastered with a patchwork of labels, attracted the eye; open, it exhaled an odour of naphthaline, wool that had been dyed and re-dyed, and slightly mildewed leather.

"We'll go to my place first, shall we?" Jean said. "For one thing, it's almost on your way, and, besides, we can see if May has telephoned or written. If you're thirsty, you can have a drink and you can pinch some of my fruit. It'll probably be better than what you'll get at the hotel."

As I said nothing, he added carelessly: "I'm not inviting you to tour the premises tonight. My little place is so much more attractive in broad daylight!"

He seemed extremely gay; he was humming. He kept leaning forward, then sitting up straight again, displaying at every moment a delight in coming home again which I could only watch, without sharing. In the old days, when we returned from a tour, Brague would begin to fidget excitedly as we approached Paris: "Dear old hole, bless it!" Even Fossette, if I had taken her with me, would sniff the first suburbs, sneezing and shaking an imaginary mane. But I? You could hardly expect my heart to soften at the first sight of the Hôtel Meurice, like a homecoming Breton's catching the first glimpse of his village steeple! With a start, I felt a familiar, comradely slap on my knee, then a gloved hand imprisoned mine as it had in Nice.

"What on earth's come over you?"

"I don't know, I'm happy. I'm very fond of my neighbourhood. I like coming back to it with you."

"I know your neighbourhood. I lived in it a . . . a long time ago."

"Really!"

The intonation amused me. It was disapproving and showed no desire for further information. The car stopped and I jumped out, without being invited to, from sheer need to stretch my limbs and breathe; it was an involuntary movement that committed me all the more to continuing this journey together. It was a dark, damp, mild night. I recognised, from very long ago, that nocturnal smell of the Boulevard Berthier, where the passage of flocks often leaves the warm, musty odour of stables and sheepfolds.

Jean lives in one of the last little houses on the boulevard. I must have visited this one, in the old days, when I was a young married woman. Yes, I am sure I have. The narrow stairs, the dining-room on the left, the drawing-room on the right. But now there is a light paper on the walls and a waxed wooden staircase that smells of furniture-polish.

"Funny, it doesn't look like a man's house!"

"Yet I've made it into a bachelor's house. When I offered to furnish it for May she told me I had a damn cheek offering her this tart's poky hole. The little house has never recovered from it!"

"Oh! A fire!"

A lovely blaze of logs lit up the room Jean had just opened. My exclamation was so excited and greedy that Jean gave me an inquiring look, his eyebrows raised and his chin thrust out in that way that gives his expression of surprise an air of disapproval.

"Of course, you don't understand. . . . No, don't switch on the light, you can see the fire better. You don't realise that . . . we're nearly in March, aren't we? Well, I haven't seen a wood fire for a whole year."

"Are you joking?"

"No. Where do you expect I'd have seen a wood fire? In the bedroom of 'good' hotels they don't even have fireplaces any more. So . . ."

I fell silent out of laziness, out of well-being, as I stretched out my hand to the fire. It was such a glorious, generous fire, the fire of a bachelor whose man-servant does not worry about expense. It made a magnificent, varied noise on the hearth; from time to time a charred twig jumped out and burnt black on the marble, like a joss-stick, sending up its thin skein of smoke that smelt of creosote and sandalwood.

I sat down cross-legged in front of it and Jean went out of the room. Was this a drawing-room? Yes, or a smoking-room. In the dancing firelight, I could make out gleaming wood surfaces, the curved legs of some charming old pieces of furniture, the dim greens of a tapestry hung on the wall, the belly of a blue vase.

But nothing meant so much to my weariness, to my trembling audacity—the audacity of a woman about to fall and watching herself fall—nothing meant so much as that fire against which I was taking refuge.

"Don't you want a cushion? I'm doing the waiting, Victor hasn't come back from the station."

Jean put a tray loaded with grapes and oranges down beside me.

"Winter fruits; a meagre supper, eh? There's some not very exciting dessert wine in this decanter and some fresh water in the jug."

"Oh! you shouldn't have bothered! Anyway, I'm going in a minute. . . ." I glanced up at him with a look that must have been despairing but he seemed not to notice and sat down cross-legged like myself, after having carefully pulled his trousers up at the knees. The dancing red light turned his face into that of a terra-cotta statue with silver eyes. He sucked grapes and threw the empty skins into the fire with a childish gravity, while I drank the juice of a split orange. Then he poured himself out a large glass of water, wiped his fingers and said "Ah!" in a way that implied: "Well, we've got to make up our minds to do *something!*"

And I suddenly realised that he too might be frightened and undecided, that his reserve, ever since the kiss he had given me, might be due more to hesitation than diplomacy. At the exact moment when I was losing even the outward appearance of calmness, a providential malice restored my self-control.

I reiterated: "Ah!" in the exact tone he had used, and I added: "That was the transitional phrase I was searching for! It leads on quite naturally to the next one—viz: "Eh! eh!" In all languages, that means: "Goodness, it's already past midnight!"

The fire was crumbling into embers; in the thickening shadow I could see the silver eyes gleaming with a slightly negroid ferocity and I began to reckon less on my host's shyness and apprehension. To fortify myself and also to insult Jean mentally, I conjured up the memory of Max, so amenable, in spite of his strength, and so honourable, even in the attack, that I was never frightened of him. Promptly, I shook the memory off with an ungrateful jerk. "Ah, no, leave me in peace; I've quite enough to cope with with this one."

This one had lain down flat on his stomach and was propping himself on his elbows, his head close to my knees. He turned his eyes towards the door and muttered, as if he had not heard me: "It's Victor with the luggage."

"So?"

"So don't move. What does it matter to you if Victor has come back with the luggage? Nobody comes in here unless I ring. Don't go, unless you really want to."

This direct challenge to my sincerity left me dumb and stupid. I really wanted to tell the truth but it seemed to be breaking up into separate strands inside me like a haycock swept away by a stream. Which one should I choose? Admit to him that his lightest word would keep me here? and that, at the same time, I felt cold and gentle, my senses asleep, very different from how I felt last night? It was all true, and all impossible to put into words.

Perhaps he guessed this, as he stroked my ankle through my silk stocking. But it was hardly a caress, it was like the mechanical movement of tracing a pattern on a material or a wall-paper with the tip of one's finger.

"Tell me," he reiterated, "tell me if you want to go?" He had crept a little closer still; I could feel his chin on my crossed knees. I looked him straight in the eyes and answered sadly, "No."

There was only one expiring flame left in a corner of the fireplace. It would sink down on to the glowing mass of pink and black embers and seem as if it were quenched for good, then once again it would escape and shoot up, flickering. Now concealing it, now modelling it clearly, it was the perfect light in which to study this man's face, so close to mine yet almost the face of a stranger. My voice had been so sad when I made my admission that it had prevented him from leaping on me; he had hesitated, then decided to adopt an affectionate, courteous tone to say eagerly: "Then you'll stay?"

With a feeble gesture, I indicated my surroundings, this unknown room in this unknown house; I drew attention to the travelling suit and hat I had been wearing all these hours and I tried to make a joke of it all.

"Honestly, Jean, you must realise that with the best will to immorality in the world . . ."

Then I abruptly broke off and reserved my strength to fight him off, for he had begun to overwhelm me; he was climbing round me, paralysing both my arms. He made himself purposely heavy, he made himself as clinging as a tenacious weed. I could not get up or even uncross my legs; I struggled conscientiously, half-pushed over backwards, supporting myself on one arm and muttering under my breath: "This is idiotic . . . this is really too idiotic!" until my simple, female sentimentality suddenly burst into that resentful, indignant cry: "You don't even love me!"

Still holding me tight in both arms, Jean raised himself up and looked down at me with a severe expression.

"Well, and what about you?"

Then he bent forward and kissed me delicately on the mouth. It was so sweet after those two minutes of struggling that I allowed myself the respite of it and let my head drop back on the carpet. How sweet it was, that naked mouth on mine, those full lips that resisted the kiss and had to be crushed a little to make them part. I wanted to stay prone like that, with my heart pounding in my throat, while the rosy fire warmed my cheek and its glow was reflected above me in two silver-grey eyes. How sweet it was, the moment of losing myself enough to think: "I am freed from the trouble of thinking. Kiss me, mouth for whom I am only a mouth." But that mouth was the mouth of an enemy whom the kiss was making ruthless, who knew I was conquered and would give me no quarter.

Arrogant, completely assured of his triumph, he displayed a barbarous contempt of methods. Hair, skirt, fine linen were all rumpled and crushed together as if he had not time to undress me. It was I who muttered, in shame: "Wait!" It was I who undid buckle and ribbon and removed pins that might hurt; it was I, lying on my back on the carpet, who made my slightly bruised body a cushion for Jean. Yet when he lay resting his head in the hollow of my shoulders with his hair tumbled over his forehead, his eyes closed and his mouth half-open, it was I who was the happier.

"Are you all right?"
"I am all right."

I seemed to have fallen from a great height into the middle of that bed where I lay prone, motionless and crushed. A fresh breeze, a ray of the setting sun came in through the open window and, every time a lorry or a motor-car passed, I saw the reflection of the water in a glass dancing on the ceiling. I felt a little giddy because my head was lying lower than my chest but I remained, out of laziness and by design, in this attitude which concealed my face and revealed all the rest.

All I could see through my tangled hair was the ceiling and the dancing reflection. Long ago, when I was a child, I used to stare at the sky like that, between criss-crossed barley stalks above my head.

A bare arm slid against my hip and I murmured feebly: "Stay still, do, you're not cramping me."

The arm raised itself to support the back of my neck and I accepted it. I nestled against this body which lay close to mine, making use of it as if it were a cushion or a piece of carpet. Then I lay still and laughed very softly.

"What's making you laugh?" asked Jean in a careless voice.

"I'm laughing because I can hear your movements. You've just stretched your arm out to the table the fruit is on and you couldn't reach it. Now you've let your arm fall back on the bed, regretfully. Tell me, isn't that so?"

"You're quite right. But come a little closer to me. You've slid right into the middle of the bed, I can't see you any more."

I moaned like a wounded person: "Oh no, no *no!* I implore you. I shall break to bits if I budge now; go on being patient."

He was silent and I went on waiting blissfully for my strength to return.

How long was it since we had rolled interlocked on the carpet in front of the dying fire? A day? A year? Only one day and that seemed so long ago. I came back today, I had lunch with Jean and after lunch I followed him into his bedroom. He did not close the window; he did not draw the curtains. How well I co-operated with him! So well that our embrace was like a harmonious wrestling-bout, planned in advance.

This is something I have never known before, this intelligent pleasure of the flesh that instantly recognises its master and responds to him by quickening for him and becoming pliant, docile, ardently reckless. It is so delightful, so easy, so totally unlike love.

At the mere impact of our bare knees, at the interlocking of our arms in a purposeful grip, I felt I was entering on hours of delight without danger. I was proud that I had given him as much as he had given me. Everything had been so perfect; I did not want our repose to be any less completely satisfactory than our pleasure. That was why I nestled comfortably against Jean and at the same time verified that his long leg lay quietly confident beside mine, neither tensing politely nor drawing away.

We had not spoken much but we had said necessary, pleasant, truthful things to each other. He had told me: "What lovely arms you have and how I like to feel you solid and heavy in mine when I lift you up!"

And I had declared to him in my turn: "How perfectly you suit me! You have a skin that's smooth and warm and dry, like mine."

And he had remained serious when I told him he was beautiful and I thought him the more modest for not protesting, since his face and his body . . .

I was imperceptibly worried as I tried to recompose
exactly the features of his face that had just eluded me
like a capricious word. Let me see . . . I could draw
the nose from memory, and the dimple in the chin. The
mouth—oh! the mouth! I knew the colour of the eyes,
and . . . No, the face would not coalesce into a whole.
Did I have to make the appalling admission I had
forgotten it?

With a jerk I sat up in the bed and bent anxiously
over Jean as if I really had been frightened I would no
longer recognise him. Thank goodness! There he was
as I *knew* him. No doubt his face had been too close
to my eyes all today, mouth against mouth, his hard,
cool nose against mine; his features had been blurred.

"Why are you laughing again?"

"I'm not laughing, I'm yawning. I feel good. Your
room smells of carnations. How brown you are on that
white sheet!"

He stretched out his limbs and let himself be stared
at. The curve of his eyelids makes him look as if he
were smiling when he closes his eyes. Very lightly, I
touched everything that attracted and intrigued me in
that exposed face; the small shaved area that makes
the hairline recede, the feminine lips, the neck that was
so young, so flawlessly smooth. So young! It was the
first time I had thought of his age, of him as a person.

"Is that a scar—there—on your temple?"

"Yes, I think so."

"And there, is that a birthmark in the middle of your
chest? A beauty-spot, if you prefer. No, let me see.
Your veins are green in the bend of your arm and at
your wrists—green, green! Goodness, I *am* enjoying
myself! How about you?"

"Renée . . ."

"What?"

I looked at him with slight astonishment when he
used my Christian name. Previously, I had not noticed.

"Do you want to get up, Renée?"

"No, what for?"

I fished out my handkerchief-puff from under a

pillow and powdered my nose and cheeks without feeling inclined for other repairs.

"What for? I don't want a bath or to comb my hair
or to go out. All I want to do is keep the good warmth
and the smell of you, to sleep in them and to wake
up when we've had enough. How about you, Jean?"

"Me too."

He rolled against me like a round, heavy tree, seeking a comfortable place with his shoulder and the back
of his neck. He closed his eyes, then opened them
again when he thought I was not looking, and it seemed
to me that those beautiful grey eyes were demanding
something of me, reproaching me for something.

"Are you sleepy? Lie there, then."

When did I last feel a man's head lying so heavily
and trustfully on my shoulder? With my nostrils and
lips I inhaled the slightly burnt smell of the harsh black
hair.

"Laughing again?"

"But I'm not laughing! Why do you want me to
laugh all the time?"

"On the contrary, I don't want you to," he sighed.
"*I* don't feel like laughing."

"You're unhappy? You're tired? You're dissatisfied
with me?"

He indicated "No" by rubbing his head against my
breast. Soon night would hide him from me, but sleep
would give him to me more completely. He would forget my cheerfulness, my companionable ease after
lovemaking. Perhaps he wanted me to be happy, but
more respectful of his prowess, more broken, more
vanquished. I was not vanquished, I was contented.

"You'll come tomorrow, Renée?"

"Why, of course I'll come."

"And the other days?"

"I don't know, how do you expect me to know?"

"Don't you want to, then?"

With all my recovered strength, I clasped the strong
body that lay relaxed in my arms.

"I swear I do."

He muttered, as if he were already dreaming. "You
see . . . I love you."

I shook him gently: "What's that you're telling me?"

"Why yes . . . you realise . . . love . . ."

I closed the beautiful, indiscreet mouth by pressing my cheek against it.

"Shh! Not that word! Goodbye. Don't talk any more. Let's go to sleep."

{8}

IF HAMOND WERE STILL ALIVE, HE WOULD LISTEN to my confidences, then he would shake his head and say: "This isn't an honourable liaison!"

I could see his long face with its big, bold nose, I could hear his voice; in short I missed them badly enough to be offended by the opinion he would have had and I defended myself against it as if he were present.

"Not an honourable liaison! And, pray, what *is* an honourable liaison?"

My old friend would have inevitably replied, with that reserved sincerity that stood up to all my rebuffs: "It's, quite simply, a liaison which, whether people know about it or not, you can feel does you honour."

His answer, which I had invented, offended me as he had offended me by suddenly letting himself die. An angry, intolerant grief had made me hot with resentment during the first weeks after his death: "To do such a thing to me, to *me*, to *me!*"

I still miss him. It is a selfish grief that afflicts me when I need not advice but intelligent, disinterested conversation to distract me from my exhausting interior monologue. When I am in that state I do as I am doing now: I resurrect my dead friend and imagine that he is talking. However, this bears no relation to a "psychic phenomenon"; it is simply a question of making the voice of Hamond speak for the conscience of Renée Néré.

There are days when, having left Jean's arms, I go away and walk along the fortifications which are beginning to show signs of green, days when I secretly exclaim: "Is this all?" Yes, this is all. "It is quite enough!" replies the languid body. How sensible it is, this contented, heavy-footed body!

A dishonourable liaison. Why cast an unnecessary slur on the ill-assorted but well-matched couple that we are? Why not throw myself into this as whole-heartedly as Jean, who is so charmingly rash as to want to live under the same roof—strangers as we are with nothing in common but physical delight? I am touched that he will not much longer tolerate the overnight luggage concealed in a "small" handbag: a nightdress and two silk slippers; nor my comings and goings between the Boulevard Berthier and the Hôtel Meurice. I am touched when I suddenly see him leave his lunch and rush upstairs to the first floor, three steps at a time. When he talks of "our future life", I shall never interrupt him to tell him: "These aren't plans for the future you're making; they're furnishing estimates." I shall not tell him that, in deciding to do what seems to him open and honourable, he risks compromising the frail—but perhaps durable—bond between us. Frankly, I like the discomfort of these sporadic meetings. I must not let him know this. I must commit myself to the same extent as Jean which, after all, is not saying much: he is only giving me a definite place in his home. I still do not know if he has finally broken with May.

All the evidence points to it and I am convinced he is no longer her lover but he has not *invited* me to know it. What is he waiting for? The installation of the new bed and the carpet the colour of silvery mouse-fur? Furnishing estimates!

Ever since our embrace in the glow of the dying fire, I seem to have been holding in my hands, in my arms, everything that Max neither could nor would give me in those days: physical love for physical love, a splen-did adversary well suited to me, a passion into which one entered, as into a secret room, already throbbing with anticipated pleasure. The preparations for our meetings would have occupied part of my days which would henceforth be idle and I can imagine how swiftly the time would pass, divided between expectations, possession and greedy memory. It is a great deal. It is enough. I have heard young women declare trenchantly: "In love, my motto is *all or nothing*." Well, well, a charming nothing, admirably presented, is anyway something.

Jean wants more, and I acquiesce, not to be outdone in generosity. The remarkable thing about our relationship is that all day we outdo each other in cautious reserve about the most trivial subjects.

"Would you like to go to the theatre?"

"Yes, I'd quite like to."

"But perhaps you don't really want to?"

"What about you?"

"I want to do whatever *you* want . . ." etc., etc.

Before we were lovers, we were not so formally polite to each other. Yet, on the other hand, what a warm urge to come close together, what sincere throwing off of reserve, if he presses his mouth to mine, if his hand caresses me tentatively! Then an inimitable confidence, if not the other. "Is that all?" Why yes, that is all. And who would not be content with it?

"What are you going to do? Aren't you coming with me to Levallois to see the garage man? The car's had a nasty bash, you know."

I made my habitual grimace and the glass in front of me warned me: "Take care! That's an expression you'll have to avoid in the very near future."

"No . . . the garage man doesn't tempt me."

"Where are you off to, then?"

"Don't know. Taking a little walk . . . maybe as far as the Meurice. The laundress should have brought back some of my blouses."

"Why don't you stay here and make yourself at home?"

I straightened the bent shaft of a hatpin and stared at Jean in blank perplexity. Why, in fact, didn't I stay where I was? There were books in the smoking-room-cum-drawing-room downstairs, a chaise-longue, the almost insipid cigarettes I prefer, and Victor, the manservant, would surround me with discreet attentions which signified: "Mind you, I'm not wild about *you*, but I couldn't stick *her* at any price". For even the silence of this Parisian servant has a common accent.

"No . . . You see, I'll get a headache if I stay shut up indoors."

"You mustn't do that, you mustn't do that!"

"I'll just go a couple of steps, then I'll come back. Anyway . . ."

I was lying. I was going to the Hôtel Meurice.

I would check my linen and spray it with scent to disguise the odour of chloride and chilled iron, I would open the papers they bring me every morning and glance through them rapidly, sitting in an armchair, with my feet on the table: I would dawdle about my room, polishing my nails and listening to the familiar music of crockery and glass being got ready for dinner that rose from the courtyard and the distant violins playing in the glass-roofed hall. Then it would be time and I would return here with a freshly "done" face, in which for some hours nothing would be lacking; on the contrary, I should have put on a little too much of everything. In fact I should do nothing bad and nothing good, but I should go to the Hôtel Meurice. It was my right, my habit, my dull and hygienic interlude. I should return there tonight, for I am not sleeping in the Boulevard Berthier—not yet. . . .

All we have experienced together is daytime sleep that descends suddenly and as suddenly departs. I am apprehensive about a whole night; it is not Jean who has anything to fear from the surprises of waking up, the revelations of the broad daylight of morning. We often sleep in the afternoon, through the sunlight or the spring rain, while down in the basement kitchen Victor raises his rat's head to the level of the pavement the moment anyone rings and guards us against the possible return of May.

May . . . a name that, ten days ago, we mentioned every other minute and that, little by little, we are eliminating from our vocabulary; a name around which a rather suspicious uncertainty is gathering. I have not written to May; throughout our haphazard intimacy we have never corresponded with each other. But I believe that, if I had been able to say to Jean: "Keep May, don't defraud her of anything but the secret hours you devote to me", this dishonest solution would have given me a very honest satisfaction. What would those "all-or-nothing" ladies, those intransigent suffragettes in the cause of love, think of me? But I am not speaking of all Love, I am only claiming my share of the . . . of . . . in fact to be allowed to keep what I have and which, for me, is so new and light-hearted, which pacifies my mind and gives a fresh, warm glow to my skin. I know all about the great transports and the great agonies; like everyone else I went through all those when I was a young, inexperienced woman. At the moment, I felt I wanted to please everybody, even May.

"Hi! . . . Renée, Renée!"

She had so suddenly appeared there in front of me, at the very second I was mentally pronouncing her name, that my first thought was to blame myself. "Serves you right, that's what comes of summoning her."

She caught me up as I was walking along by the Tuileries. She had jumped out of an orange motor-car, a curious little vehicle with a bare, rounded behind, like one of those sick hens that has lost its back feathers. I did not flee, but while May was running after me with constricted little steps, I imagined myself lying down, well-guarded, in Jean's smoking-room. I sighed and resigned myself to the shock.

"So I've found you, you quitter!"

Quitter? She sounded effusively pleased to see me, not angry, did that mean she knew . . . everything—everything except about me?

"Come in here, I've got some very serious things to tell you."

She dragged me into the melancholy garden, naked of grass and greenery, and, to fill up the silence, I made such remarks as were strictly necessary.

"Well, honestly . . . You always drop from the sky like a thunderbolt. Where have you sprung from?"

It was as much as I could manage. May's scent, her arm tucked in mine, the sudden physical contact with *Jean's mistress* disturbed me in a most painful, unexpected way. Most intolerable of all was feeling that

rounded arm clutching my own, knowing it was the
arm of Jean's mistress.

"Very serious things, I tell you. You look marvellous. I'm pale, aren't I?"

She was as pink as an azalea, but it was a pinkness
that doubtless concealed an authentic pallor. I thought
she was looking very pretty. She seemed to me prettier
than ever: a regimental ribbon encircled her straw cap,
her neck was bare under her jacket that was at once
skimpy and loose, a strand of hair gleamed like a
streak of gold braid on her temple. Never, no never
had her twenty-five years so deliciously glamourised the
faults of an idiotic fashion. I could think of nothing
else. I had to make a mental effort to recall myself to
reality and tell myself, "You have taken this young
woman's lover. She might be brandishing a weapon in
her hand, instead of a rolled umbrella!" I felt no terror,
except one of subtle repugnance whenever May pressed
my arm closer as she talked or laid her ungloved hand
on my hand.

"You know what happened?"

"Happened when?"

"After you departed from Nice?"

"No. . . ."

"Jean left me."

"Yes. . . ."

"You knew that? Was it Masseau who told you?
After I returned here—I'll spare you the details, shall
I? Jean came to see me twice, as charming as could
be."

"Ah!"

"But that's not paying him any compliments because
every time he becomes very charming, it's a bad sign.
I wasn't taken in, I got the letter five days ago."

"What letter?"

"*The* letter. The letter to say it's all finished."

"Ah! And didn't you do anything?"

A bitter wind was sweeping the terrace and blowing
stinging dust in our faces. May clutched the brim of
her hat and my eyes were streaming. But it did not
occur to us to go anywhere else.

"What d'you mean, I did nothing? Ah, you're talk-

ing of . . . of revolvers, laudanum, navaja, all that bag
of tricks! Just imagine! With a boy like Jean!"

"What's so special about him?"

May turned her back on the yellow Seine and leant
on the balustrade. Clinging to her hat, with her skirt
plastered against her knees and her stomach she looked
like a passenger on a yacht heeling over in the wind.

"If you like, he hasn't anything special about him,
yet, in one sense he has everything. He's a man, that's
all. The more you see of men, the more you tell yourself they're all alike in everyday life . . . then when
something happens, some quarrel, some misunderstand-
ing, you stand there gaping at them as if you'd never
known more than one. Don't you think there's some
truth in that?"

"I'm sure there is."

"I had that feeling with Jean even more than with the
others. I even had it all the time with him."

"One would never have guessed it."

May gave a sidelong smile, her golden lock blown
into her eye; she had taken my sarcastic remark for a
compliment.

"I had it all the same. He's a fellow you're all at sea
with. Rotten with pride, to begin with."

"Is he?"

"Goodness me, yes. When he's made a mistake, just
try rubbing his nose in it and making him own up to
it, you just try, you'll be astonished! His Lordship
knows everything, His Lordship's so bloody cocksure!
Because His Lordship's ruined himself a little bit in
motors, a little bit on the stock exchange, and in politics too—for hardly long enough to mention it he had
a government job in Ille-et-Vilaine—a little bit here,
a little bit there—he's more infallible than the Pope."

"Just fancy that!"

"And secretive, my dear! When you think he hasn't
got a bean, he's got money. When you see him flinging
cash about in handfuls, it means he's on the rocks.
Always the same thing—pride! Like his way of saying
nothing sometimes when I was telling him off good
and proper. That way of smoking without saying a

word, holding his cigarette in his teeth and sticking his chin out."

I could not imagine anywhere where I would feel worse than I did where I was. The wind, May's words, the shame of listening to them, all these combined to produce a physical misery that was a blend of migraine, sea-sickness and cramp in the stomach. Alas! I could not doubt that this woman was suffering. She was suffering as much as she could, to the full of her small capacity.

". . . And to smile like that, you know, as if he were gazing right through the wall at something you couldn't see. 'Joan of Arc and her visions', as I used to say to him. . . ."

But what right had I to assess the quality of her suffering? And what was I doing here, listening to humiliating confidences? The most trivial of my questions and exclamations that invited or prolonged an answer of May's were as bad as listening at doors or prying open a letter.

The only honourable words, the brave exclamation: "Don't say any more, Jean is mine now," refused to cross my lips. . . .

"Let's walk a little, this spot is impossible. Mind you, all these things I'm telling you about Jean aren't crimes. *He's* ever such a character, too. When a woman has said of her lover that he's conceited and 'superior' and rather underhand and none too generous, that doesn't make him a scoundrel. But there's something worse about Jean."

"Whatever's that?"

The wall of the Orangery sheltered us. Quick, during this respite of the wind, let me bend down to catch the last vile whisper, the best one, the one the little deserted mistress was keeping for a *bonne bouche*. How cold I was!

"The worst thing about him is the way he f——s off."

"Yes?"

"He f——s off like no one else and you never get him back. I can talk about it now because the first effect's worn off, thank God. But what Jean did to me is no more and no less than he did to Marthe Byse, famous star as she is, no more and no less than he did to Madame . . . oh hell, my memory for names . . . A widow, that pretty blonde? . . . well, it doesn't matter. He f——s off, that's the frightful thing. When you chuck each other, it's after a scene, isn't it? . . . Or coming unstuck, little by little? Well, my dear, *he* f——s off in the middle of a sentence, closing the door behind him, or else he goes out to buy cigarettes and you never see him again except in the form of a farewell letter, very well written, simply marvellous. . . . I don't know if you're like me but that affects me much more than the gentleman who stages a big scene: 'Since we must part . . .' Jean's way is the worst way of f——g off because, mark you, he doesn't do it like the gentleman who snatches your purse and disappears in smoke, oh no, not at all! You write to him, you ask him to come and see you and someone turns up who's called Jean, and is wearing a suit and tie you know very well. You recognise the stick, the cuff-links, even the sound of the voice. But the gentleman—he's f——d off so completely that you stare at him, you open your eyes as big as saucers and you ask yourself: 'Well, honestly, *did* I sleep with this man or didn't I?' Listen, I'm not spiteful, but I'd like to see the face of the woman who's pushed me out when Jean f——s off again! . . . Now it's raining. We only needed that. Come along, I'll run you home in my car, a yellow car . . . that's appropriate or I'm a Dutchman. But a character like me isn't superstitious. The car and the person who's waiting in it is a try, a feeble try. . . ."

"I can't, I've some shopping to do, under the arcades."

"Let's run then! I offer you half my umbrella."

"No, run on ahead! I've got nothing on that rain will spoil. Run! Yes, yes, I'll telephone you. . . ."

She ran with short quick steps, her skirt hitched up round her knees like a little pair of knickers. She went off, lightened by all the load she had left with me. Ah, it was then that I wanted to speak, to own up, to come out with everything I had been choking back a few minutes earlier.

"May!"

Luckily, she did not hear. A taxi came by; I managed to gasp out the address in the Boulevard Berthier: "And drive fast!" Suppose, in my absence, Jean had "f———d off"?

[9]

JEAN! . . . AH! YOU'RE THERE!"

"Why of course I'm here! What's the matter?"

"Nothing. Just imagine, I let myself get caught in the rain, so I came back here instead of going and dressing myself. Too stupid of me."

"It's never stupid of you to come back here."

"But I wanted to make myself beautiful. And here I am again just as you left me."

"I should hope so! You look very much like a certain traveller who sat there on the floor one night. I like you."

"As much as she?"

"Better."

Slowly, I pulled myself together. By talking, by saying pleasant nothings, I concealed the anxiety that had sprung up when I left May and that had grown, on the way back here, into an irrational panic: "Jean has gone . . . I can feel that he's gone, I'm convinced of it."

May's words had followed me all the way with the malevolent force of a *spell:* "He f——s off and you never get him back!" The narrow house, blinded with shutters, looked to me deserted, and I called out "Jean!" in the voice one uses in nightmares.

There he was, very much present, very much alive, between the fire he was stoking up for me and the lamp topped with a shade like the luminous roof of a little pagoda. The twisted feet of the armchairs reflected the flame and the silk curtains were a mellow, sumptuous red.

"What's the matter with you? Odd for a woman who was supposed to be taking a couple of steps, to arrive in a taxi, looking as if you'd returned from heaven knows where."

"I think I've caught cold. Oh! it's nice here, in your home."

"There are hazel-hens for dinner and a Viennese tart —a big, heavy tart."

"Really? What luck! And what did he say, your garage-man?"

"He said, seeing the crack that splits the door from top to bottom: 'The door's cracked'."

"You can't hide anything from him."

He wandered about the room, pushed forward an armchair, pulled the curtains and "tidied up" with the good grace of a bachelor host. As he passed me, he stroked my knee and caught hold of my ears, like two handles, so as to kiss me better. His hands, his body, his smooth cheek—they were all warm and firm, all infinitely, preciously alive. I contemplated him admiringly: so close, so free, perhaps all mine, perhaps already lost to me.

"And . . . how many days will he take over it?"

"Will who take over what?"

"Why, the garage-man."

To Jean's surprise, I let a long time elapse between his question and my obvious answer. A very long time indeed, during which I stalked round him, taking a bitter pride in seeing him so intact, so little touched by life, so well-equipped to hurt, as I might have said yesterday. Today, I said to hurt *me*.

"Help me, Renée! Look how unhappy those roses look laced up in their tight string corsets."

"It's not worth the bother. Roses from Nice, they only last two hours in a room where there's a fire."

"Two more hours of beauty in front of you—don't you think that's worth having?"

I flushed in the shadow and gave him a vindictive look, but he had spoken in all innocence.

"There! Is that all right?"

"Very nice indeed. But I had to ask you! I'm always

surprised. Come and sit on my knee . . . surprised to
see how few feminine ways you have."

"Go on, tell me I ill-treat you!"

"You don't arrange flowers in vases, you don't pull
the table-cloth straight when it's crooked, you don't
pat the sofa cushions. You sit down, you cross your
legs."

"Don't exaggerate!"

"Well, anyway, you behave like a lady paying a call
and that annoys me."

"Me too."

"Aren't you my lover then? Don't you want to belong to me as I belong to you? There are days when
you humiliate me with your hurry to get undressed
before and get dressed again after. Days when one
really wouldn't think that you love me, but that you're
using me."

I listened complacently, without the least resentment.
Sitting on his knee, I gazed at him from close to,
breathing in the smell of his hair that tongs daily
scorch a little; at last I had him! "I have him," I
thought. "Let that be no more than the affirmation of
my senses—not a thought, not a hope which the future
is already withering. . . . Oh, let it express only the
pleasure of this hour and not commit me further than
here and now!"

He sulked, with more grace than conviction, but he
was not very pleased. He would lose his temper, if I
egged him on.

I caressed him with growing melancholy, for I was
beginning to realise that his changes of mood had very
little effect on me. Jean in a temper, or Jean disdainful
and sarcastic, or Jean crafty and a little cautious as he
always is when he turns very gentle, what did it matter,
provided it was Jean? The marvel of his *presence,* the
unutterable security of all one's senses.

"Understand me!" he said impatiently. "You only
seem interested in what I take from you, not in what
I am!"

"And you?"

He lowered his brows like an animal and his whole
forehead seemed to come down. I guessed from the

relaxing of the knee I was sitting on that he wanted to throw me on the floor.

"Me? You know perfectly well that I . . ."

"Say it!"

"I've said it to you already! I said it first!"

"That could have been a reflex. There are moments when the expression 'I love you' is no more than an involuntary nervous twitch."

We laughed, half-angry with each other. I had no scruple in contradicting him, even in bad faith. I was hungry tonight for everything he could give me; lies, obstinate perplexity, offensive gesture or too tender look. Had I not had this identical conversation long ago with Maxime? It was a distant echo that died away if I listened, a memory so faint that it cast no shadow on my present.

Nothing in my past dares impinge any more on my present. Why? Why should this utterly fresh Jean, often still as hard and closed as a tardy oak-bud, enjoy this outrageous immunity? Outrageous, because it does something worse than merely protect him; it rears up in front of him, not a faithful likeness of Max, but a distorted, almost comic picture of him. I see a Max who looks stiff and awkward, with his features drawn geometrically inside a rectangle, like the faces in Sadi Carnot's old caricatures.

Though Jean is neither handsomer nor better than Max, I never compare the two men to Jean's disadvantage. The only excuse I can offer for this is the mysterious, obtuse, feminine objection: "It's not the same thing."

He was there, close against me. I held him in proud silence, as he leant heavily and confidently against one of my breasts, crushing it with his weight. We had learnt already that whenever our minds or our consciences awoke and defied each other the only thing to do was to clasp each other tight and be silent. Embracing gives us the illusion of being united and silence makes us believe we are at peace.

"I'd like to know the evil you think of me," he sighed.

"Guilty conscience!"

"No, but I'm listening to you thinking. Your breathing's uneven, it stops when you come to a cross-roads of ideas. And when you turned your face over on the cushion, your eyelashes gave a quick flutter that scratched the silk."

"Not bad, not bad!"

"It isn't, is it? I'm so intelligent! Is something worrying you?"

"Yes: you. Do you want to know what I'm thinking? I was thinking I shall never have the courage to go back to the hotel tonight."

Almost imperceptibly he tightened his arms round me. He did not even look up but I could see a smile of delight slide down from his eyelids to his mouth. He relaxed and grew heavier, as if he were already on the point of falling asleep. I did not regret having spoken. A little sooner, a little later, the ordeal of the long night and of waking up together awaited me. And tonight I felt so cowardly at the thought of being alone in a darkness that would echo till dawn with May's voice: "He f——s off, and you never see him again."

Dinner passed quickly: we chattered with unwonted coherence and sparkle. It was as if, by using the excuse of such things as an antique sideboard and a monogram on some silver to document me about his family, Jean wanted to give me a bigger share in his home, to *invite* me more urgently into it. The way he said "My father" in a tone of impatient respect, like a schoolboy kept short of pocket-money, made him seem amazingly younger.

"How old are you, Jean?"

"Ssh! I've stopped admitting it for the past two years!"

He was joking, but I promptly imagined that he was concealing his age out of delicacy, to stop me from making comparisons . . . so I did not dare insist; I remained silent, feeling a little shaky.

"My blessed father, I can't get out of spending three days with him next week. Including the two journeys that mean I'll be away five days. If I missed my mother's anniversary, the Autocrat would have a seizure. Will you find that odd, five days without me?"

"I don't know, I can't very well imagine myself, at this moment . . ."

"What will you do with yourself all that time? Who will you go and see? Your family—your friends?"

It was the first time he had shown any direct sign of interest in me, or at least of a curiosity that was not purely sensual. Taken aback, I stared at this young imperious face that was questioning me; a family . . . friends . . .

"You know, I haven't any relatives left since my sister-in-law Margot died."

"And friends? Haven't you any friends?"

I mastered a shaming sense of being a wanderer with no one belonging to her and defied him.

"Indeed I have! I've got Brague. And I also used to have a little dancer but she's travelling abroad at the moment. An unmarried mother called Bastienne."

He was about to say something insulting, then changed his mind.

"Well . . . don't let's think about that five days ahead. Anyway, I'm not sure I won't take you with me."

"If I'd like to come?"

We laughed, and our eyes caressed each other, not very frankly. *He* is born to please without effort, to seduce, and to make his escape. *I* . . . I am like the grey mare my father had; a good cut with the lash did not frighten her but the shadow of the whip on the road, beside her ears, made her crazy with terror.

He brought his chair closer to mine and shared my dessert.

"Do you split oranges in two? *I* peel them and sugar them."

"Sugar on an orange, how revolting! I'll make you fruit salads in the summer, you'll see I'm an expert."

"I absolutely forbid you to do any such thing! Fruit salads have always made me think of . . . of dessert rejected by an intolerant stomach!"

Every time we disagreed, we were seized with immoderate gaiety. And suddenly I was stupid enough to say: "One thinks those little things don't matter a bit. All the same I used to get furious in the old days at the mere sight of my husband dipping his bread in his soup."

But Jean was not in the least interested in my husband. He had heard the clock strike half-past nine and he gave a stretch and yawned with an excellent imitation of common bad manners, showing the whole fresh interior of a well-furnished mouth. A splendid red jaw that could bite up anything. He caught my eye and the expression in his own changed, to an urgent, unsmiling gaze that said: "Come . . ."

He was asleep. He does not sleep as he does in the day time. He can sense, through his slumber, the long night ahead and the chill that precedes the late dawn of March; he sleeps in stern immobility, covered right up to his shoulders. He breathes very slowly. I could see him dimly by the light of the street lamp outside, for the window was wide open. I breathed in, as if I were in the country, the smell of wet grass and mist; a cold air that seemed pure and that made our amorous bedroom chaste.

He had left me a wide place beside him in which I dared not stir. I felt tired, forgotten until he woke up, but patient and peaceful. He no longer knew I was there. Once, I touched him very lightly; he drew his arm away with a childish, irritable gesture.

Nothing had changed. Only my inability to sleep gave a touch of solemnity to our first night whose delights equalled those of our afternoons; nevertheless it was a "first night". Before that night lay the past sealed off for me, but what did I know of our future?

Did I even foresee a future, as I kept my submissive vigil, careful not to disturb Jean's rest? I do not know, but I kept vigil because it was the *first night*. I kept vigil as any woman, raw or experienced, might do who is apprehensively beginning life or beginning it afresh at the side of a sleeping man.

"Goodbye for a little while! You've got your handkerchief, your key?"

"I was sure you'd forget it! Victor, bring down the key Monsieur left on the dressing-table."

"I'll be back early, you know."

"I hope so."

Jean studied himself once again in the looking-glass in the hall and once again smoothed his hair with the gesture of an actor settling his wig.

"Leave your head alone! It's ugly enough as it is. This fashion of plastered-down hair!"

He did not believe a word of it and his face expressed an earnest complacency, an unsmiling satisfaction that prevented his vanity from being odious. The piece of mirror that reflected me beside him seemed to be of a darker glass, greenish and warped.

He came back late this afternoon, exclaiming: "I'm dining with the Autocrat!" and tearing off his jacket and tie the moment he got upstairs. The dress I was putting out ready to wear for dinner with him remained on its hanger, holding out its two short sleeves as if it were saying: "There's nothing we can do about it. . . ." For the pleasure of following Jean and assisting at his toilet, I had stopped attending to my own, and now I saw myself in a loose dressing gown, with my hair in becoming disorder. But my figure, beside the streamlined tails, the starched shirt-front, the pale, clean-shaven face, looked sluttish and untidy; there was a heaviness about it, an indefinable air of voluptuous maturity.

"Do hurry and get off, Jean!"

"Yes, but I want you to be sorry for me."

"Because?"

"Because I'm dining with the Autocrat!"

He held out his sulky mouth one last time, before jumping, on one bound, down the steps that led to the street. I laughed and shrugged my shoulders, and, in spite of myself, I thought that he did not affect this boyish manner with May. With May, he spoke sharply and raised his hand to her, and it was May who acted like a little girl; only May was twenty-five.

The motor drove off. I remained for a moment in the doorway, leaning out and smiling as if he could see me. Above the mound of the fortifications, the sky was still a little pink and against it the black trees

thrust up their swollen buds, just on the verge of opening. Neighbours, peaceful inhabitants of this ill-famed
Boulevard, were calling their dogs and strolling about
bareheaded, like villagers, before leaving the place to
problematical "apaches". It was a very mild evening,
without a breath of wind. I could not have chosen one
that better suited my desire to be alone.

For some hours, Jean will be away. And, though
I kept saying over and over again: "Be off with you,
you'll be late!" he did not sense how much I wanted to
get rid of him. He did not realise how well chance had
served my purpose tonight, for I have a purpose. The
way I hurried over dinner was sufficient proof of it
and so, now that I have shut myself up in my room
again, is this face I see in the glass the face of someone unscrupulously plotting a crime? Yet I do not want
to write secretly to anyone nor, in spite of that hateful
look in my eyes, do I want to kill or to steal; I want
to be alone; if he were to come in unexpectedly at this
moment, or if he were hidden behind the curtains, I
should scream. I should scream like any other woman,
surprised by her lover when she is day-dreaming alone
in her bedroom; scream with terror and rage and blaze
up with the chaste wrath of an outraged priestess.
Suppose he were to come in and find me something
worse than naked—find me altered beyond recogni-
tion?

I have been living here only a month. And never did
mistress move in with less commotion; three trunks of
clothes and underwear, some papers in a box and a
beauty-case. It was all done so quickly, so simply, that
a sceptical lover would have suspected the expertness
of long habit. But Jean, mistrustful as he is, is not a
sceptical lover. The day I arrived, I shyly set down my
two essential pieces of furniture on the pretty desk in
the bedroom: a fountain pen and a very ancient little
Chinese knick-knack, a polished jade fruit, so worn
that it seems to be melting away but exquisitely smooth
to the touch.

And straight away I had begun my initiation into an

existence quite unknown to me; the only one that, under a surface of unconventionality and illusory freedom, involves outdated customs and an almost oriental dependence: the existence of the *kept woman*.

When the kept woman, like myself, has no family and no intimate friends, and is brave enough or heedless enough to entrust herself entirely to the man whom chance has selected for her, she may find her new life a mixture of pleasures and mortifications. She may have the impression of being simultaneously a convalescent in a nursing home, a novice in a dissolute convent—or a harem—and a "trusty housekeeper" burdened with a thousand domestic cares. Idleness gives me a taste for arranging things; Jean's daily absences now that "the Autocrat's" state of health involves his spending some hours every day with his family oblige me to make each of his returns a little festival; flowers on the table, some delicious fruit just in season, or the sudden appearance of a euonymus hedge in the little neglected garden. . . .

After all, the good fairy who looks after nomads keeps me from being impatient and bad-tempered by whispering in my ear: "This will last as long as you want it to, and no longer." No longer . . . so I reassure myself and bask in the present with the belated improvidence of a passionate woman to whom love was miserly in the bloom of her youth. I have grown a little fatter, I savour my food with pleasure; like Jean, I sleep long hours. In the daytime, my preoccupations are more or less the same as Victor's, the man-servant's: "Is Monsieur going out with Madame? Or without Madame? Has Monsieur come home? Is Monsieur dressing tonight?"

The first days, during Jean's absences, I made my way back to my usual eating places; the little Italian restaurant where the ravioli sizzles with butter and piping hot cheese, and the brasserie whose hot sausages and velvety beer Brague so highly commends. But I could no longer enjoy them in quite the same way, with the frank pleasure of a greedy old bachelor. *"One doesn't go to such places all by oneself!"* Jean would exclaim. "*One* doesn't deliberately give the impression, when *one* is a woman like you and *one* has a lover like me, of being reduced to sauerkraut and beer dives! Gracious, you've got a house at your disposal and a cook who's not too inefficient and yet off you go traipsing all over Paris", etc., etc., etc.

On the first rainy evening, sitting all alone in front of my ravioli, I rebuked myself with the docility of a happy, malleable animal: "Gracious, I've a house at my disposal, a cook who's not too inefficient", etc., etc. . . . and I admitted Jean was justified on every count.

If I dine at a restaurant, it is with Jean. If I go to the theatre, it is with Jean. In the old days, when I was legally married, I was allowed to have outside acquaintances, but the code of "living in sin" is far more stringent. To accompany me, I have a lover, Jean, or a bodyguard, Masseau. The same code regulates my comings and goings so exactly and to such a strict minimum that it amuses me; I am secretly flattered that such rigour should dictate the actions and behaviour of an ingénue of thirty-six, and when I risked observing one day: "But when you were May's lover, I don't think you . . ." I promptly received the stiff answer: "May didn't live with me. And besides, May was May and you're you."

"This will last as long as you like and no longer. . . ." I accept my new condition with interested curiosity. I am contracting the habit of hasty acquiescence and of childish fibbing. I content myself with what satisfies other women in my position, the free time Jean procures me by going out.

Realise this, you who say you love me: the most loving mistress turns away from her lover during certain hours which she mysteriously arranges should come and which she cherishes in anticipation. The most beautiful woman, if you perpetually spy on her, will not survive undamaged. The most faithful one needs to hide herself, if only to be able to think freely.

"Freely! To be free! . . ." I am speaking out loud to try and make that beautiful faded word come alive again and shimmer with the green of wild woodlands, echo with the beat of wild wings. In vain!

You pretend to love me; this means that all day long I must bear the burden of your anxiety, your watch-dog vigilance, your suspicion. Tonight I am not off the chain, but it has slipped from your hand and trails behind me so that I do not feel the pull of it.

You pretend to love me, you do love me. Every minute your love creates a woman better and more beautiful than myself whom you force me to resemble. I put on, along with your favourite colours, the tone of voice and the smile you like best. You have only to be present for me to give a miraculous imitation of all the characteristics and charms of my model—all that I dread is certain hours like this one when I suddenly want to scream at you: "Get out! My princess's dress and my radiant face are going to drop off simultaneously, get out!" This is the moment when the cloven hoof is going to appear under the hem of the skirt, the twisted tip of a horn under the silken hair. I am possessed by the demons of a silent, inner Sabbath. I must curse and reject the gentle shape in which you have imprisoned me.

It is growing late; I must have been alone for a very long while. How many times have I paced to and fro in front of this mirror? Each time I pass, it shows me my guilty face with its false, sidelong, anxious smile. One shoulder droops slackly, the other is hunched up to the ear as if to ward off an unexpected blow.

Just now I squatted down in front of my reflection in the attitude Jean dislikes: with my arms crossed on my knees and my breast crushed against them, I rocked myself like a sick bear.

I remember having frantically scratched my head like a real flea-riddled gipsy. I must also have fixed my gaze on the glittering belly of a little copper vase that glows in the shadow like a red-hot poker, for I can still feel its luminous point hurting me between my eyebrows. And during that time I must have been utterly blank and forgotten to think.

A little shock roused me, a disagreeable little mental shock: "What is Jean doing?" With marvellous promptness, a mental picture followed the question. It was not Jean in the arms of May, or bending over an unknown woman; it was Jean all by himself, walking along gaily, his nose in the air, exactly as he might be walking about the streets at this moment. He too is alone. Why hadn't the thought occurred to me before? And why should "Ah! so he is alone!" seem an amazing, alarming discovery? Why shouldn't he be alone? I have wanted it often enough lately, haven't I? Whatever imbecility has replaced for this whole past month my fear of seeing him "f——off?" I make use of him, of his house, of his table, of his car. I retreat, at his expense, into lairs of solitude from which I defy him and where I sometimes almost forget him. In fact I behave towards him with that selfish stupidity which women agree to call masculine. "There are two kinds of love," says Masseau: "Unsatisfied love which makes you intolerable to everyone and satisfied love which makes you idiotic."

So Jean is alone too. Intoxicatingly alone, like a student staying out all night, or deliberately and sullenly alone, resigned to finding the same woman at home as yesterday?

Let me be just—and to be just is already proof of great humility in a woman—whether our adventure continues little or long, all I can reasonably count on is Jean's resignation, for that is all I deserve. For a month I have been giving myself to him each time he wanted me, each time we wanted each other. The rest of the time, what does he know of me? Am I Venus or the Queen of Sheba that I need only lie on a bed to satisfy this beautiful young man to whom I owe more than he owes me? The rest of the time, I study him, without sounding his depths and I judge him as if he were still May's lover, not mine. That counts and weighs too, the *rest of the time,* and it adds up to a great many hours.

When he has been reticent, I have judged him as empty. And, when he has questioned me about myself, I have fobbed him off with a would-be superior irony, so whose fault is it, if, instead of being here with me at this moment, Jean is walking the streets or sitting on a lighted terrace, and breathing in the soft night air with a face that does not belong to me?

He does not know that I am kind and loving, that I have the makings of a stalwart friend. I attribute to him the defects which make a certain type of man successful: duplicity, unscrupulousness, laziness; but it is I alone who impose them on him like some flashy adornment that would suit his slightly brutal face.

I think my profound mistake is that, up to now, I have never tried to dissociate Jean from the idea of sexual pleasure. When the appetite is gorged, the thought of sex arouses coldness and indifference. Famished, it wants nothing but what appeases it.

Jean . . . oh, obtuse brute that I am! There is a Jean who is not Renée's lover, a Jean who is neither mysterious nor sexually exciting. And that Jean—so young still, with his caustic laugh—has matured and developed from the boy he was in the past and whom I never knew. Jean's thoughts, Jean's soul—did I really believe these had any place in our brief exchanges of words or in the frenzied silence of our nights?

I have insulted this lover, out there alone in the soft spring night, restoring his own identity; I have insulted him by giving him my body and supposing that this was enough. He has returned the insult. I only hope he will not come home at this moment; I would be quite capable of crowning my folly by being absurdly effusive. Far better he should go on wandering, alone and pure, as remote from me as if he had never met me.

When he returns, I shall be in his bed and perhaps I shall be asleep. I am aware of worse dangers now than sharing my sleep with him. My slumbering shell belongs to him and does not succeed in forgetting him. Without leaving the deep realms into which I plunge in my dreams, I grip his hand tighter or make room for his head on my shoulder. Nestled against him, I sleep easily and naturally. Alas, he is not here yet and already he is taking possession of me. That swift, hastily averted glance is the one he finds attractive.

Standing upright, with her feet together and her bosom held high, with a growing radiance mounting from her lips to her forehead, the woman you wanted, the woman whom perhaps you love, resurrects. You may return.

❧[10]❧

"WHAT'S THE TIME, MASSEAU?"

"Quarter to."

"Quick, gather up the cards. Leave that ashtray, I'll empty it myself. And pass me that glass of anisette, there, on the table. I'd no idea the days were drawing out so much. He'll say again that the place reeks of stale tobacco smoke."

"That window's been wide open all the time."

"That makes no difference, he's got a nose like a hound. You've let a card drop on the floor."

" 'He that is down need fear no fall'," quoted Masseau sententiously. "I'll pick it up. It's a nine of spades. 'Troubles'."

"Get along with you, you old sleepwalker! What's that I hear? Is it he?"

"Why no, it's a taxi. For one thing, he wouldn't be coming from that direction."

"Why? He goes to the office every day now because the Autocrat isn't getting any better."

"To please him?"

"Yes . . . no . . . to replace him."

Masseau gave a little snort. I said: "After all, he's his father's son, he's the one who'll succeed him. You seem to think it funny that he should go to the office."

"Not in the least, my dear, not in the least. Better than just anyone, as good as the next, no worse than Tom, Dick or Harry."

"Shut up!"

"I can form a very clear notion of banking."

"Can you? Oh, *really,* Masseau . . ."

127

"And to prove it . . ."

He turned up the points of his detachable collar in the old-fashioned way, pushed up his tie and tried, by puffing out his cheeks, to make one believe he had dewlaps.

"Laffitte!" he exclaimed.

"Did Laffitte look like that?"

"I don't know. I hope so. Give me three francs and twenty centimes which you lost at the game of bezique. Thank you. May God repay you a hundredfold."

"That will make precisely sixteen louis. That knock, is that he?"

"No, it's the ice-man."

"You'll stay to dinner?"

Masseau cast an avid glance at the folded card-table.

"I'll play you for my dinner. If I win, I'll stay. And if I lose, you'll keep me to console me."

Frustrated of his game, he followed me into the dining-room where I absent-mindedly make little adjustments to the laid table, pinching the stalk of a flower, spacing out the glasses. The solitary tree in the garden, a chestnut, pressed its leaves against the bare window-pane; the electric light bleached them to the pale green of a young pod.

"Look, Masseau, it's a pink chestnut. You can see the colour of the buds—already!"

He agreed, nodding his melancholy bald head. The scalp showed yellow under the parsimonious strands of long hair, patiently divided up to cover it evenly. I hastily averted my eyes which were used to lingering caressingly on Jean and looked instead at the open door.

"It isn't he," said Masseau, with sardonic acuteness.

"He . . ." Masseau had not spoken Jean's name. And I too say "He" like a woman obsessed with her man. But I am ashamed that we should say it in hushed voices, with a slightly degrading complicity, like Victor the manservant, leaning over the food-lift and whispering down to the invisible cook: "*He* says the sweet was a failure. *He's* noticed the fruit dish has been stuck together."

An intolerable ringing broke out in the hall.

"Oh, that infernal telephone! I'd smash the beastly thing if I had my way. Hallo, is that you, Jean?"

I knew already what that far-off little voice was going to tell me—Jean's voice, clear but with a twang in it, as if he were joking.

"Hallo! Yes, it's me. Listen, don't wait dinner for me, they're keeping me here at Papa's. He's not too good tonight."

"Ah?"

"Yes. Can you hear me? Hallo! Whatever's the matter with this line? Hallo . . . You know, I'll be back immediately after dinner. Are you alone?"

"No. Masseau's here."

"Oh well, if Masseau's there . . ."

"What did you say?"

"Nothing. Goodbye for the moment!"

"All right. Goodbye for the moment."

Savagely, I hung up the detestable instrument whose function is to receive and to bring bad news. Heard on it, the voice seems to become pregnant with meaning, and to betray unspoken thoughts. "Oh well, if Masseau's there . . ." What did that mean? That Jean would take his time and come home at two in the morning? I am beginning to know his "Goodbye for the moment!"

I turned out the light in the hall—an old, economical habit I have never entirely broken. Besides, the face of a disappointed woman who is mastering her irritation is not a very pretty sight. . . .

"Let's sit down and have our dinner, Masseau. Jean's dining with his family."

To make the table look symmetrical, Victor had put Masseau in Jean's usual place. An unspeakable depression, nigh to tears, overcame me at the sight of his face opposite me. Instead of the firm, low-browed face with its well-cut mouth and discontented nose, I had to look at the sharp, twitching features of an ageing, almost bald man, riddled with nervous tics. . . . I wanted, oh, how I wanted at that moment!—just to be May or any other little "character" who could relieve her feelings by childish tears, by smashing plates, by screaming alternately: "I want Jean, now this minute!" and "I'll never see him again, he makes me sick!" But exhibitions of that kind have to be left to the Mays of twenty-five summers who can laugh after their tears, display a little pink nose and lovely wet eyelashes and look as artlessly fresh as a wild-flower. For Renée Néré, tears are a disaster.

"What are you looking for under the table, Masseau?"

"An animal, to give it something to eat."

"You know perfectly well there isn't one here."

"I do know it, and that surprises me."

"Oh, nonsense! Imagine starting all over again to train a puppy or a little cat, getting fond of it, dragging it about from hotel to hotel. . . ."

Masseau blinked faster. "What do you mean, from hotel to hotel?"

"Yes, I know there's no question of hotels at this very moment. But one never knows, we aren't chained to each other for life, Jean and I. We haven't sworn eternal fidelity, thank heaven!"

I felt I was being rude and clumsy, using that false voice, putting on that unconvincingly cynical expression. My off-handedness might have deceived an idiot but not Masseau who, embarrassed by all that I did not admit, gave up trying to make me laugh. I do not confide in him but he has become a habit with me. I remember that it was he who brought me to Jean and, in my familiarity with him, I display a little of the shameless unreserve one might feel in talking to a eunuch or an unscrupulous nurse.

It seems endless—a dinner at which nobody eats. Yet Victor kept going to and fro with an affectation of silent alacrity that got on my nerves. His discreet rat-like face and his airy footsteps were at such pains to convey to us that we must pay no attention to his presence that we saw and heard nothing but him.

"Coffee in the drawing-room, don't you think, Masseau?"

A moment or two later, I collapsed in my favourite soft armchair.

"Ouf! Alone at last! When I say *at last,* that makes three dinners without Jean I've regaled myself with this week. What can one do? That man makes a positive cult of his family!"

"His father is ill," said Masseau gently.

"Oh, I know he is. But even if you told me his father had golden hair and wore divided skirts, I shouldn't make a tragedy out of it."

"In that case, I shan't tell you any such thing," said Masseau, still very gentle.

"Do you think I'm asking you to, my good man?"

"I do think so, and I shall confine myself to answering you this: One of two things, either I am the repository of Jean's secrets and I ought not to betray them or I am ignorant of them, in which case, in spite of all my desire to strike death into your soul, I can only keep silent and, at this point, enrich my great *Treatise* with a few notes."

"What great Treatise?"

"Hush! . . . and affirm my superiority at bezique by winning some money off you."

"But you won't go as far as helping me or taking my side! If I asked you to do something for me and tell Jean . . ."

"Nothing doing!" interrupted Masseau with such vehemence that some of the strands of hair came unstuck from his scalp. "Nothing doing!" He added, almost in a whisper: "You realise, my dear, that opium is expensive."

I understood. I understood only too well. Poor Masseau! I was quite aware that Jean gave him money to buy the drug, exactly as he might have given him good cigars, with the serene unscrupulousness of a friendly poisoner.

"Obviously . . . my dear old Masseau, I'm not the person who'd be officious enough to tell you: 'Give up smoking and get cured'."

"Any more than I would advise you: 'Leave Jean if you're not satisfied with . . . the state of his father's health. Or make him happy once and for all.' But that last suggestion is beyond the powers of an intelligent woman!"

"I know. What you mean is it needs those of a maid-servant who's been promoted to her master's bed. So we'll make Jean marry his cook."

"Like me," said Masseau, without moving a muscle. "But there is no urgent hurry and we have time to think only of you. What you have to deal with is a boy, who is fundamentally rather simple. Arrogant from birth and brought up to be despotic, because he always saw Mama tremble before Papa. A little humiliated by having dabbled in everything and not stuck to anything; a little young to be good and still deluded enough to rebel at the idea that woman can occupy the most important place in a man's life and heart. To sum up, Gentlemen and valued colleagues, we have occasion to offer our warmest congratulations to our town-council. Let us now affirm, with one voice: 'This is a great day for the Republic!'"

"What on *earth?*"

"It's the peroration of one of my speeches at Saigon in 1893. As you see, it's as good as new."

I listened, smoking a cigarette. I nodded approval and thanked him with a connoisseur's screwed-up glance.

"It's very good, you know. The 'instructions herewith' are first-class. You haven't added the 'Directions for use' which, in any case, was unnecessary."

"Why?"

"Don't know . . . Have an idea . . . Jean is charming . . . So am I . . . We shall remain charming . . . on condition we don't exaggerate anything. . . ."

I had lit another cigarette, an indispensable property when one is giving a classical performance of carelessness, slightly cynical detachment and civilised immorality.

I said, between puffs: "Charming, I assure you. That's exactly why I want to preserve a memory of our . . . adventure . . . that will be worthy of it. No chain, not even a chain of flowers—it's so ugly, a withered garland! Something I'll call 'an infallible instinct' warns me that Jean and I have everything to gain by going back to being just good friends. We rushed into bed together . . . excuse the expression . . . too quickly, almost without knowing each other and . . .

you'll understand me when I say there's a certain un-
predictable temper, certain oddities of character, certain . . . in fact certain things that I can't accept."

I stopped short and blushed to the roots of my hair:
that last phrase was May's private property. How often
she had used it in the days when, having been soundly
thrashed in private, she redressed herself in public,
glowing pink with freshly-scrubbed pride.

As if to make the analogy all the more cruel and
before I had had time to hear the car drive up, there
were steps on the sanded path and Jean opened the
front door. The next moment, he was in the room.

"It's you!"

My loud, startled exclamation embarrassed all three
of us and made Jean grow red.

"Yes, it's me. It's me once again. Goodness, to hear
you scream like that when I come home, anyone would
think it wasn't me you were expecting!"

He was wrong, but I took advantage of his mistake.

"You realise I wasn't expecting you so soon. You
look tired. How's your father?"

"Better. Well enough to have become intolerable
again. And to think I'll be like that at his age! What
did you two have to eat tonight?"

He sat down and stretched. He talked. I knew he
would not pronounce the words that would unite or
sever two destinies. But there he was, as he said, "once
again". I could feel Masseau's eye on me but even that
sarcastic little eye could not prevent me from following—in the most dog-like sense of the word—all Jean's
movements. All I did was to raise my head a trifle
and turn my gaze and my body towards the man who
was talking. But I knew that every movement of mine
was as significant as the tilting of a flower towards the
sun or the yielding of a ribbon of seaweed to the curve
of the wave.

There he was, the man whom just now I had wanted
to leave—but did I want to leave him? The contrast
between my lying words a little while ago and the
burning truth of this moment was so violent that I
shivered. There he was, fidgeting or sitting still in his
usual way, and everything seemed simple between us

and around us. Yet I knew that he was more hidden
from me than a god in his cloud. From now on, he was
interposed between me and all the rest of a clear
universe in which he alone was opaque. There was no
piercing his mystery which existed only for me and
for which I was almost wholly responsible, since he
was my lover. Love is that painful, ever-renewed shock
of coming hard up against a wall which one cannot
break. We might have remained two friends, walking
parallel with each other on either side of that crystal
barrier, without realising that it divided us. But love
was going to impel us towards each other and I
trembled lest I, the more fragile one, should be the
first to shatter myself against it.

Sleep eludes me and you lie asleep beside me. You
go on sleeping under the lamp I have just turned on—
Psyche's torch does not awaken you. Are you dreaming? No. I cannot see on your cheek or your brow that
quiver like the reflection of running water, that ripple
from the well-spring of your being that betrays the
swift passage of a dream in your deepest consciousness.
You do not dream when I am there. It is as if you do
not want to. How well you defend yourself! This is
the time when I wander all round you as under the
walls of a locked palace. Where can I reach you? What
breach can I open in your smooth, unlined forehead?
Speak, avid mouth, and tell me in your sleep what
you will never say in the brightness of day! Tell me
what they hide, those sly smiles of yours, like the
smile of an animal caught thieving and still licking its
chops. I have so often seen you with eyes that are
suddenly empty; eyes paler and blanker than a vast
stretch of sea without ships.

Leaning over you, I catch back a fluttering piece of
lace against my breast for fear it might brush your
cheek, and I scarcely breathe. But can you not hear
the buzzing of my angry thought as it beats vainly
against the deaf shell of your ears, against your insensible nostrils and mouth?

The time is past when I used to admire your capacity
for sleep and smile whenever I glanced at you! Beside

you, I could read and think undisturbed; pleasantly
aware of you like a treasure lying strewn on the bed.
I could forget you and then recollect you again; you
were neither more precious nor more galling to me than
my other possessions.

Something has happened between us which has
poisoned all that. Is it love, or only the long shadow
love casts before it? Already I can no longer see you
as luminous and empty.

I measured all the danger, that day when I began to
despise what you gave me; a gay, facile pleasure that
left me ungrateful and frivolous, a slightly ferocious
pleasure like hunger and thirst and as innocent as they.
One day, I began to think of all that you did give me;
I entered into the chill shadow that travels ahead of
love.

And here I am, humiliated, spying on your sleep.
Oh, my treasure, strewn there on my bed, can it be that
I disdain you because I am beginning to love you? Oh,
Beauty, can it be that I prefer the soul perhaps un-
worthy of you, that inhabits you? Are there words now,
Beauty, that dull the lustre of your name—such words
as jealousy, betrayal, fidelity?

Once again, I have consumed the night in contemplating you, you who were my pride, my succulent and
unloved prey. I can see the time close at hand when
the growing shadow of love will have covered me, the
time when I shall be still more humble, when I shall
think such deplorable things as: "Does he love me? Is
he deceiving me? Heaven grant that I know all his
thoughts!"

I am not wholly deluded, not yet. I still have enough
strength to leave you—if I want to. You wake up
slowly—I know so well how your eyelids reluctantly
open, showing a thin, wavering line like the streak of
light on the horizon that heralds the dawn. . . . And
you would find yourself alone, you would pick up this
ribbon that ties my nightdress. . . . Never again would
you hear that quiet, very quiet song, always the same,
that I sing for myself alone and to which you listen
behind the closed door.

No. I stall stay. A kind of obtuse heroism keeps me here, on the verge of my ruin. I shall stay. Sleep while I lie awake, calmly imagining the best fate that could befall you! A merciful death that would petrify the image of my new love for ever in your pose of impenetrable sleep.

❦{ 11 }❧

N<small>O, I DON'T AGREE WITH YOU."</small>

That was all I had said. He was politely silent and I stared at the sea, dotted with islands. We had not quarrelled, there was nothing to quarrel—or even to argue—about. That was all I had said, yet it was enough to make us both feel we had parted for ever.

At our feet lay a narrow sandy beach, still wet between boulders that had been bored through over and over again by the waves and whose base was blue with tightly packed little mussels. Beyond it, the ebbing tide was uncovering bare, peaked rocks. As far as the eye could reach there was not a single detail to mar or ruffle this Breton landscape; not a storm cloud in the sky, not a ribbon of wrack or a fringe of flotsam on the edge of the sea, not a house on the coast except this one, Jean's. It is a low, grey house, with a sparse wood behind it and, in front, a blaze of red geraniums and a scanty field that slopes down to the sea and blossoms with wild roses, stiff, fragrant pinks and gorse-bushes through which the wind whistles.

It is a perfect place, right at the edge of the land from which it seems to be trying to escape and take refuge in the sea which is gradually wearing it away. High tide encroaches on it till there is nothing left but a narrow strip of sand, rocks and grass, then, as it ebbs, it concedes it an insecure territory of beaches and reefs that never have time to dry. It leaves behind tiny, populous lakes whose bitter water is incessantly agitated by the claws of crabs and lobsters and the swishing tails of sea-perch and shrimps.

We came here last week. We arrived at the hour of twilight, a twilight whose rosy glow seemed to be shed equally by the setting sun, its reflection in the sea and an early-risen moon riding high and pale in the sky. We were not proof against the intoxication of the sea air which, those first nights, disturbed our sleep, quickened our blood and prolonged our hours of lovemaking under the febrile blue light of the full moon.

Everything was new to me, or unrecognisable; the salt on Jean's lips and mine, the noonday smell of the west wind which had passed over half-opened shellfish and that of the land wind, sweet with the scent of warm hay; the seaweed, the clams with their quilled valves, the sand-eels like mother-of-pearl whips, the furious crabs; the water that rose up and clasped, first one's ankles, then one's knees, in two heavy, icy bracelets. Last of all there was Jean himself, gentle and half-naked, like a faun. Every day he went down to the sea and I watched him admiringly as his step sent rippling shadows over his back and that magnificent muscular V that one sees in beautiful statues.

But already he was wearying of the holiday routine, of the sand clinging like a warm shroud to the drenched skin, of the silent siesta, almost blank of thoughts, under the softly-flapping canvas awning. Already we were being invincibly drawn back to our awareness of each other and the words I had just uttered seemed to be those he was expecting.

"No, I don't agree with you."

I do not know whether my tone made it sound more portentous or whether it was Jean's expression when he heard me say it that transformed it into a sentence of doom.

We fell silent and he lowered his eyes, for a curious kind of dignity forbade him to look, like myself, at the ebbing sea and the huddle of red rocks. That path of light, opened up between two clouds and running right to the horizon, was the path down which I was escaping. To have followed my gaze would have been, for Jean, almost tantamount to giving in and acquiescing. He would not give in so soon.

I had just offended him gravely, since I did not agree with him.

"Jean, are you angry? You think that I'm wrong?"

He protested, without raising his eyes: "Not in the least! I bow to your decision."

Yes? Or was he being crushing?

Goodbye, goodbye, I do not agree with you. Once again we were separated; far, far away from each other. By stretching out my hand, I could have touched his hair on which the salt water was slowly drying. A moment ago, our dark, drenched heads had emerged from the sea together and now we were so far apart. Goodbye, goodbye! Was it for the last time?

For I could feel that he despaired of me. One word, and our life in common had become intolerable to him; he would give up the journey he had planned and the tempting night that lay ahead. It was not that he hated me, no: he was shaking me off.

I did not speak. I used the exasperating weapon of the weak and the calculating: patience. I behaved as if I had forgotten Jean's existence. But he was not entirely deceived. During our first quarrels, my excellent imitation of the unself-consciousness of an animal which knows it is all by itself used to delude him completely. But he soon learnt that I merely wanted to offend him and he took offence. Now, perversely, I take care to talk and to keep silent just enough—enough to ruin everything. Instead of consciously trying to bring about our complete union, I want this to come about through a catastrophe, through some providential disaster and I keep incessantly piling up the clouds over our heads. My poor lover, how can I make you a sign across this barrier my false pride is building up between us, and what chance remains that you would recognise the sign?

You excuse everything in me which in any way resembles you. You overlook my lying, my bad temper and a certain frivolity that breaks out in bursts of wild gaiety for, in any extremity, whether of pain or pleasure, I depend on you. But today, you are utterly baffled, "I don't agree with you".

I said those words. I think I uttered them with a

theatrical slowness, with a kind of deliberate security to show that they were something more than an evasion, that they implied a retreat, a return back to what Jean sometimes calls *my people*.

"*My people*" is an expression he uses to designate all the unknown side of my life. He says "my people" as if he were talking of a hostile tribe whom he instinctively hates. It is about "my people" he is thinking with deep mistrust at those moments when his eyes ask me so clearly: "Where do you come from? Who are you?" when he seems to be searching in my shadow for the indecipherable, paler shadow of so many vanished forms, the shadow of so many strangers who have made me in their image. They, too, "*do not agree with him*". Is it solely because of them that, in moments like this one, Jean gives me up in despair?

Passion—the only thing that brings us together—lay dormant, withdrawn into some dark refuge—and there we were confronted with each other, two people who were neither friends nor relatives. Anything—invective, wounding words, even separation—would be better than our dismal game which can go on for ever, in spite of Jean's quickly-exhausted patience: if he is the dog, I am the cat at the top of the tree.

Jean, my ill-loved one. . . . Once again, our thoughts were running in opposite directions. I was going back bitterly to the time when I called my brief adventure love with a Passer-by. But he must have been going back to the days of my first perfection and reliving them, adorning them with a posthumous poetry. He must have been dreaming of the first weeks of our love when he suddenly began to believe in me, in my permanence, in my total submission, and repeating the words he found to flatter my pettiness. My opaque silence was elevated into "pensive wisdom" and the laziness that he irritably sees today as the inertia of a worn-out gipsy impressed him as regal.

So we sat there, patient, in front of the island-dotted sea. Once again, we were vaguely expecting that some chance would bring us together again as just now it had separated us. Or else the impure tide of desire which had been secretly mounting would sweep us both away till it stranded us once again on a barren shore. What point have *you* reached? Have you finished heaping abuse on me? Go on, magnify all my defects! When you have made me an enormous, blackened monster, loaded with more evils than a cloud swollen with hail, you will have gone a long way.

I myself have reached the symbolic halt in the journey which brought us here; I am back at that beautiful day on the mountain. Right on the top, standing on the red ruin, you drank in the blue air that whistled between the stalks of lavender. With genuine enthusiasm, invigorated by a little reading, you raved aloud over the open expanse, the towns, the villages, the shape and the clearly defined limits of a province girded with mountains and hills. You traced it through its history and you searched its soil to find the footsteps of its conquerors.

I was there, close beside you, and the grip of your strong hand on my arm stressed your words. I was there, rebellious and out of tune with you, far more interested in the magical appearance and disappearance of a lizard, in a tuft of marjoram swaying under a hornet buried in it, in the cry of an invisible shepherd. I was observing the mountain with the narrow range and the eye for small, sometimes subtle details, of a woman and a short-sighted woman at that.

When you realised this, all your excitement dropped dead and, as you stared at me dubiously, I felt at once far away, yet dangling in your clutches—small enough for you to carry me off yet heavy enough to impede your flight.

Were you thinking, as I was, of that day on the mountain? Were you counting, beginning from that day, the hours when we crazily supposed we had wrenched ourselves apart?

I did not know. But your silence despaired of me. Under your outraged stillness you were conscious of a regret that made you feel like a waning god, the furious regret of not having created me.

Today, I escaped from him by a path through furzebushes that clawed at my dress. I reached an echoing shelter in the rocks, inhabited by a whirling wind. Down below, among the long narrow reefs, the ashen sea was boiling and writhing with the violence of a dammed-up stream.

From the height of my breached tower, I could spy on the house, draped with dark, glossy ivy. Jean was down there. He was reading, with his forehead rammed between his fists like a schoolboy. He would not come; up here I had leisure to calm myself. I was chewing a wisp of bitter little grass that made my saliva taste of box-leaves and turpentine. The wind dried the spray on my arms and cheeks and my fingers were rough and green from twisting the spikes of broom that had brushed against my hands all along the path. On me and in me I bore the smell and the savour, the bitterness and salt of my jealousy.

I was—if jealous was the right word—jealous, festering from something Jean had said, a terrible thing he had said hesitantly, as if he were spelling it out: "I'm afraid we don't need each other enough. . . ."

At that rather cowardly "we" that did not dare to be "I", I ran out of the house. When I returned there, he would give me all the usual things: the reassuring word, the convincing caress, the sworn promise. He would find it easy to exculpate himself because he feels blameless and because he still believes—poor simple man!—that fidelity should be sufficient to engender trust. He will not know, he must not know, *in what way* I am jealous. For him, jealousy means physical unfaithfulness, picking up a crumpled letter—it means the hope of winning back a disputed possession. To be jealous is to see all the time behind a woman, the shadow of a man. I envy him.

But I, *I* . . . if he does not need me enough, what have I been doing all this time and what future have I with him? He is more necessary to me than air and water, I prefer him to the brittle possessions a woman calls her dignity, her self-esteem. Only his single, solitary figure rose up before me on the ravaged field of my memories, rose up between me and the short waves of the absinthe-coloured sea. I could forget his last love and the face he kissed before mine; I could thrust all that away with careless impatience. He was all that I gazed at, all that I reviled. I was jealous of him alone.

I do not know how or when this thing first came over me. I remember one day turning round and finding him standing behind me, and, all at once, it was like seeing him for the first time. The sight of him startled me into a peculiar rage, a mixture of a sudden premonition of losing him and the humiliation of being more his than he was mine.

I suddenly saw him, with his typical stance, stooping forward a little like a man about to break into a run; with his voluptuous way of breathing in the scent of a flower. It was then that, muttering angrily to myself, I began to realise—too late—how much he meant to me.

Too late! Already, had he known it, he could have tyrannised over me in scandalous immunity. Had he known it, he could have made imperious demands on me and found my generosity inexhaustible. He could have expanded and ripened in me as in some beautiful province that nourishes every fruit. Had he known it, I could have been, according to his whim of the moment, the warm silent mouth or the sisterly arm or the friendly voice of a wise adviser. Everything—I could have been everything, flawlessly and effortlessly, and you have no inkling of it.

At this point my jealousy surged up again, inflamed by an imaginary notion of poetic justice, and burst into a bitter lament: "What I have been to you, *you who do not need me enough?*—you are destined to be for another woman." Does she exist? That is irrelevant. But I foresee that I am preparing a lover for another, a love whose splendour I alone know; a love in the image of my own love for you which I hide from you."

"I perish at the thought that one day you will equal me, you whom I might fill to overflowing. You will equal me, only to overwhelm another woman with love, or to live with her as I live with you. When I create you as you will be then, you dazzle me. It is as if I took off all my secret jewels so as to assess their worth better: when I see them glittering on you, I weep to see how precious they are."

"I left you just now because I had not the strength to hurt you. I have come, by a thorny path, to this dungeon of rocks where the wind lashes me like my sorrow. There is nothing left in me, above me, below me but churned-up sea, crumbling stone, gusty clouds. This tempest of sea and wind, this debris of shattered rocks might have been created by my own inner confusion to honour and glorify you, you who have just appeared in the doorway of the house. You look so small in the distance, a slim, tiny, clear-cut shape—tiny and terrible."

❧{ 12 }❧

THE DARKNESS IS EBBING. A FAINT WIND STIRS THE trees, bringing a green smell of trampled grass. Behind the plane-trees, the mound of the fortifications is emerging from the dusk and the sky is taking on the colour of a field of blue flax, the subdued, slightly grey, slightly melancholy tint of a summer dawn over Paris.

A lean tom-cat, on the nearest bench, is savouring the peace of this cool hour and taking no notice of me. I make so little noise that he does not know I am watching. Now and then he raises his head and gazes at the sky with a blank, poetic gravity, untroubled by wariness or fear. Both of us are waiting for the dawn.

It will be hot. It will be a long day, like yesterday. Paris is already humming regularly and mysteriously with a murmur like the sea at low tide on the margin of a flat beach. For me, it will be a very long day. I know in advance all its phases; already, as a deserted woman, I have my fixed routine and now and then I take a curious interest in my plight like an incurable invalid who distracts himself with his illness. I know that in a few minutes, in an hour at most, I shall have got through what is perhaps the worst period of my day, the one that follows my brief sleep.

Before I wake up, before the lucid moment of remembering, there is a confused whirl in my mind in which shreds of dreams mingle with a hazy reality; my whole being defends itself and refuses to *know* Jean is gone. This very struggle and the pitiful unconscious movement I make to huddle myself together and hide in the hollow of the bed only bring back more clearly

145

the memory of everything. Then I give up struggling;
I meekly get up from my bed and go over to the
window, pink with an August dawn or blue with heavy,
beneficent rain.

Then I take to pacing up and down the room, from
one wall to another. I bow my head for this is truly
the awful hour. I use what little strength I have left
to stop myself from beating my head rhythmically
against the cool wall of the bathroom, to stop myself
from moaning "Oh!" every time I take a new breath.
I am patient. I move noiselessly about this bedroom
that does not belong to me, I avoid looking at Jean's
portrait which the triumphant dawn is bringing to life
again on the mantelpiece. I give a wide berth to the
table on account of the cigarette-case Jean has left
behind there, a leather case whose smell I suddenly
caught the other day as I passed. I had not time to
master myself and the next moment I was nothing but
a lost animal, whimpering over its master's scent it
had picked up again.

And then I go over to the window and lean my
elbows on the sill in an attitude which is already
habitual and I begin to suffer as a matter of routine,
to suffer in the same way as yesterday and all the days
before. I do not want to weep: I look at the avenue,
the scorched grass, the dawn colours brightening in the
sky: I am interested in a passing flock of sheep kept
together by mute, panting dogs. Sometimes I smile as
I watch the games of the prowling cats; why not?
Everything I see is registered against the solid background of my grief but my reactions to it remain the
same.

The "pain of absence". . . . By dint of compulsively
repeating, over and over again, those three words,
always the same, always at this same window, I have
come to distort their meaning in the strangest way.
Because I always lean sideways on the bar that is too
low and obstinately persist in bruising my left side on
it, I identify the "pain of absence" with a physical
pain, here, in my side below the heart, in that place
I crush against the wooden bar, tenderly, as if I
cherished the hurt.

The pain of absence. . . . It is such a simple form of suffering. How far removed I feel from the base tumults of jealousy and its homicidal madness! Everything is so simple in my mind, as simple as my grief; he was with me, he has gone. I have no other desire, no other hope, except for his return. If only he would come back, loving or not. If only he would come back. . . . If only he would come back.

A thrush whistles softly. The voices of a thousand dusty sparrows accompany his song with a sustained twitter that can barely be called musical, a cool noise like wet gravel being swept. The sky and the pavement reflect the same fleeting whiteness before the sun rises; it is that virginal moment the gardeners in my native province, who took care to pick the fruit firm and cold, used to call strawberry hour.

Strawberry hour. . . . There are certain old expressions like this which touch off some mysterious spark in us and kindle our imagination. Quick, let me carry this one while it still rings in my mind with all its delightful associations back to my crumpled bed. Perhaps, for a little while, its magic will fend off the, alas inevitable, return of a ghost. Due to the strain of standing so rigid here by the window, I am shivering as if with cold. Suppose I am going to fall ill? But, madmen do not fall ill, nor do those who are being inwardly devoured by a single obsession.

Slowly I go back to bed and defiantly get between the sheets of this bed in which there still lingers a vague scent that is not my own. Now I have to force myself not to give in to anguish, not to upset the sad equilibrium of my day by a storm of tears. In any case, the sun is rising. The first metro train will soon be passing, then there will be the milkman's knock at the basement window, then at last the step of the first postman. He will bring me nothing, nothing from Jean. But, after him, there will be other postmen whose footsteps I shall listen to as they approach and recede, footsteps that punctuate my day with rising and ebbing tides of hope.

So in turn will come all the other hours to be worn away; bath-time, luncheon-time, the siesta behind the closed shutters, the dragging, spun-out walk, dinner with Masseau and then the night. Once again the night, the arid night of a Paris summer; what would I not give for a film of damp mist, for a ground fog smelling of dew and earth? Once again night, solitude, insomnia, the inevitable awakening.

Sometimes I tell myself: "There is no reason why all your days and nights should not go on like this to the end of your life if he does not come back." But the suggestion smacks too much of ordinary commonsense to frighten me: all I look forward to is the wildly improbable . . . his return.

He has been gone a month. He left me with a kiss: his family was expecting him in the country; his father, ill or not, had summoned him there. I said to him: "Mind you write and let me know how you are!" in the gaily incredulous voice one uses to a forgetful young brother who is going away for a week. He replied: "As if I wouldn't!" But, as I watched him crossing the broad pavement, his whole back was lying. I called him back: "Jean! No, I'm wrong; I thought we'd forgotten to put your mackintosh in the car."

He turned round quickly and I had time to read the expression on that handsome, obstinate face and in those eyes, almost green in the shade of the plane trees. They showed treachery, impatience and a kind of affectionate cowardice, the cowardice of those from whom the sight of the hurt they inflict draws tears.

If I myself had been sincere at that moment, I would have held out my arms, I would have burst out with those extravagant words that come quite naturally to lovers: "If you go away, I may die. Truly, truly I may just cease to exist without you, because I love you. You couldn't do anything more appalling to me than what you're doing by just walking away from me. Forgive me for having taken so long to realise it."

He went off, calling out one last time, "Au revoir!" He was lying. I went back into his house and I began to wait for "the letter" as May said, "the letter that means it's all over".

Nothing has come, not even that, against which I

might have defended myself, pleaded—if necessary, threatened. Nothing, except two ambiguous telegrams, whose content in itself was trivial, and which were sent only to find out whether I was still there, whether I was still obstinately encumbering the house that was not my own. When the second arrived: *"Be kind enough ask Victor send riding clothes and boots. Much love."*, I "translated" it and meekly put on my hat to go over to Batignolles and look out the few pieces of furniture I had kept. They were piled up in the sinister gloom of a two-roomed "flatlet" that I use as a furniture store. I stared at them, I wiped the dust off the cracked glass of a pastel with my finger, and I shook my head, saying almost aloud: "No; I can't", and I returned to Jean's house.

The next day I went to the Hôtel Meurice and asked for one of those blue or cream or peppermint green rooms which had been old haunts of mine for three years. And while one of the staff was vaunting the recent improvements in the hotel, and calling me "Madame Renée" as he talked, I listened with horror to the violins in the lounge moaning out a hackneyed waltz. From now on that languorous waltz would be entwined with too searing a memory.

That moment was one of my worst and weakest. I was conscious of an icy terror—the fear of the unseen snake you have nearly trodden on and which escapes from under your foot, the fear of the hole with crumbling edges, the reminder at every step, every moment, of what I had lost. "No, I can't." And I returned to Jean's house.

Here, nothing distracts me from Jean. As to the waltz, I sing it myself.

"What's the matter with you?"

"With me? Nothing."

One of us would sometimes ask the question, sometimes make the reply; we had almost reached a point where our conversation consisted entirely of these few words.

We could no longer communicate except through uneasiness, for nothing is exchanged in the sexual act. Speech gradually withdrew from us as the sound of shouting and singing, all the warm, irrelevant noise of living creatures must die out on a frozen planet. Our love which had begun in silence and the sexual act was ending in the sexual act and silence. One day, I dared to ask Jean: "What are you thinking of?" and then promptly began to laugh and talk without waiting for his answer; I was as much terrified of a lie as of an admission. I could feel him fluttering at my side, beating his wings and on the point of escaping from me like a bird already airborne. Yet every night brought him back to me and not once did I find the courage to repulse his desire. He made love to me only in total darkness and in sombre silence and I imitated his mute activity. At the height of the struggle he wrested an angry pleasure from me, and abandoned me afterwards, sickened. Then the ditch between us, hollowed a little deeper by the weight of our two bodies, separated us for the rest of the day.

I reached the point of looking with envious admiration at the sealed letters the post brought him, thinking that there were people in the world who corresponded with him, who exchanged ideas and plans with him, who talked to him about the future. People who, although they had met and known and loved Jean, continued to live and think and act normally. I even envied May, who had got off so lightly. Retracing our short, abrupt path, I woud deny that a strong healthy love could be born, after a few weeks of false comradeship, from a kiss on the nape of the neck. Yet at the same time, the memory of that heavy kiss would bow me down more than ever. But since this is love, Jean, why does it not make us happier?

It is too late to ask myself that question now. I did not dare ask *him* "why" and perhaps he realised it. I did not dare. He was merely the man to whom I displayed myself naked.

He has gone. Does May know? Has he seen her again? She was only a poor little innocent prophetess, yet, now that fate has put me in her place, I think of her harshly. I accuse her and her kind, her and her predecessors, of having exploited Jean without knowing I existed, of having moulded him for some unknown woman, in no way like me, whom he is pursuing through all of us. Is he seeing May again? My pulse does not beat faster, no offensive picture rises up before me: the idea of betrayal plays so little part in my torment. This is neither nobility nor disdain, but simply the result of an odd sense of security. I do not feel any woman between Jean and myself. He has gone off exasperated, unable to bear our secretive, overcharged silence any longer but there is no one but myself in his mind. This does not rouse any glimmer of hope in me, it only spares me a slightly keener pain by relieving me from the wretched anxiety of *comparing,* of seeking and finding, in some young, well-made passer-by, reasons for despising what beauty remains to me. Although it is beginning to fade, my physical charm does console me, though I do not deceive myself about what is going and what is still left. If grief consumes one, as they say, by now I should be an old woman. Yet, in spite of insomnia, in spite of the tears I cannot always restrain, in spite of an obsession more wearing than tears or insomnia, I keep myself up to the mark, ready, from the moment I get up to the moment I go to bed, for any surprise appearance. Even Masseau himself has never seen me look slatternly.

Nowadays, I cherish this curious friend. I suspect that Jean writes to him or at least that he writes to Jean. If he is no longer the messenger, almost the go-between, he once was, I hope that he is still the spy and that he reports my words, the look on my face, my elegant decline, to Jean. I resurrect every night for Masseau. Out of dignity, I take care not to display my misery to him, but I act, almost unconsciously, in a way to stress this dignity of a deserted woman, too proud to show her feelings. I play bezique gaily—a little too gaily. I am hearty—a little too hearty—at dinner. I act "naturally" as they say in the theatre, with the "naturalness" of a juvenile lead who affirms, biting his lip and clutching his breast, that he is "perfectly all right".

Play-acting—but if I did not act, if I let myself go,

Masseau would find me waiting in the doorway, pale and trembling, crying: "You've seen him? He's talked to you? He's mentioned me? He's coming back? Tell me! Tell me! Bring him back to me, bring him back to me! Let him know, through you, that everything will be easy, everything will be a joy, if he comes back. Tell me that if he comes back, I shall feel him coming, that if he were only out there at the end of the street, I should know it as infallibly as a parched leaf knows it is going to rain! Tell him that, but, above all, tell him to come back because I am getting weak and all hollow inside and I am afraid of dying without him."

"Hallo, dear old Masseau."

"Pray accept, Madam, the assurance of my most cordial esteem. P. Masseau."

"Literally?"

"Literally. Why, if one writes as one speaks, not speak as one writes? I once—but this is a tale of my brilliant youth—put myself under a cloud with Madame Auberon—for having thought I was talking to her when I was writing to her, so my note ended: 'Well, so long! See you next week!' Is that what's making you laugh?"

"No; it's your hat."

Masseau was reflected full-length, from his straw hat to his shoes, in the hall mirror which always seems a little tarnished on account of the meagre light that filters through the fanlight and the greenish canvas that covers the walls. I saw myself standing beside him, as I had stood beside Jean when he was going off to dine with his father and I waited for the sharp twinge of memory—a contraction of my sides as if I were plunging into a cold bath—to subside before continuing my laugh.

"What's wrong with my hat?"

I had no idea. It was a straw boater. In the hand, it looked like any other boater. Neither did Masseau's tie differ intrinsically from any other tie nor his jacket from any other jacket. But on him the unobtrusive cloth, the inoffensive rice-straw and the conventional tie took on a malevolent life of their own. At a sign

from Masseau, would they not come running—the hat
bowling alone on its brim, the jacket limping on its
empty sleeves, and the tie wriggling like a hissing
snake?

"General Boulanger!" Masseau curtly informed me,
as he stood planted before the mirror. "Bad business."

Turning to me and touching the lymphatic swelling
above his beard, he consented to explain, "When I look
like General Boulanger, it means my liver is out of
order."

"The heat, no doubt?"

"Yes, the heat of the summer, the summer of 1889
which was terrible in Saigon."

He rubbed his hands and I preceded him into the
smoking-room.

"It's nice in here, isn't it?"

I was lying. Everything in it was sinister, behind the
half-closed shutters. A place without a master, a deserted woman.

"Very nice," agreed Masseau, sitting down.

He has a manner of his own of sitting on one but-
tock, like someone who has come to ask a favour.

"The days are drawing in already," he said in his
old lady's voice.

And, for some reason, just those words threw me
into a frenzy of despair which I succeeded in hiding.

"Why yes, my dear Masseau. One must expect that
now. Anything new?"

He blew his nose before replying and I sat rigid and
crazily tense, saying to myself: "If only he will take
a long time blowing his nose! If only he will leave me
for just another moment the possibility, the hope that
there is something new! If he was very malicious, he
might leave me in doubt and not tell me till the end of
his visit that *there is something new.*

But he was not very malicious. He answered at once:
"No, nothing. And you? No news?"

"No news." And I added weakly: "Why?"

Masseau raised his writer's hunched shoulder higher
in token of impotence and I grew bolder.

"After all, whatever you say, he really might . . .

Just common politeness. And even common rudeness, yes. I'd infinitely prefer that—the gentleman who writes: 'Look here, I've had enough of this!' After all, Masseau, I'm not a woman who . . . I mean, you understand."

"No," said Masseau.

The fact was I was searching for words like a foreigner. I did not want to give any trace of lyrical expression to my grief.

"I mean, he had nothing to reproach me with."

"Yes, he had," said Masseau.

"That's perfectly ridiculous! Besides, even if he'd been dealing with a . . . a woman like May . . ."

"He is," said Masseau, "dealing with a woman like May."

I opened my mouth to protest, but Masseau's attitude reduced me to silence. He had seated himself like a fakir and his little yellow hand was raised in command or in blessing. From where I was sitting, I could smell his breath, the breath of a man who hardly ever eats.

"I am about to speak! I am about to say imperishable things! I am overwhelmed with a burning desire to tell you a fable. Once upon a time there was a man in the valley of Bois-Colombes who was returning to his home. As he approached, he heard an appalling din of screaming and drumming going on inside his house. He blasphemed and stopped up his ears as he crossed the threshold. There, a filthy stench offended his nostrils; he blasphemed and stopped up his nostrils, then he called to his wife: 'Wobad,' he said, still keeping his nostrils stopped up, 'Tell me where this filthy sdench ad this did cobes frob?' The wife smiled and said: 'The stench is this unctuous cheese, all runny under its rind and the din is your son who is playing at being a soldier with his trumpet and drum.' Then the man glorified Allah and exclaimed: 'In truth, my son was born to be a warrior, to beat the drum and to sound powerful blasts on the trumpet! And, as to the cheese, pearly drops of ambrosia cannot equal its rich sweat whose very odour makes the mouth water!' Then he sat down at the table, cut the cheese and embraced his son."

"And then?"

"That's the end. It's a fable."

"Obscure, Masseau."

"If it were not obsure, it would not be a fable. Obscure, comma, dash, but the meaning is accessible, even to a feminine brain. Jean is the turbulent son, Jean is the odorous cheese."

"You're trying to make out that I ought to find everything he does charming, just because *he* does it? That's silly."

The oriental story-teller, now embellished by a little copper paper-clip that pinched the bridge of his nose, shook his head.

"It's not so silly as all that. I am trying, with the aid of a drum and a Pont l'Évêque in prime condition to make you realise what love is."

"I was waiting for you to say that!"

"You're waiting for me to say something else. And you might have waited a long time but for my weakness of being interested in Jean. Do you love him, woman-like-May?"

"I . . . Yes, Masseau."

"And he loves you, forgive me, he loved you? Now, now, keep calm. My child, remember that a doctor is like a confessor. And a confessor is like a doctor. In any case I am neither a doctor nor a confessor. Ha! Ha! Let us continue. Have you written to him?"

"Of course. Very little. Only once at length, last month."

"And what did it contain, your esteemed of the ult.?"

My nerves were on edge. Two troublesome little tears pricked my eyelids. I let myself be probed with the tense docility of a dog whose wound is being dressed.

"I can't remember now, Masseau. That I was unhappy. That I was astonished at his behaviour. That he ought not to have treated me like that. That . . . that one has dignity as a woman."

"Henough! Henough!" yapped Masseau. "I was sure of it!"

He uncrossed his lean legs, re-tied the lace of his shoe and said coldly: "You can stew in your own juice. I'll leave you do so at leisure."

After three steps towards the door, he came back.

"*Your* unhappiness, *your* misery, *your* loneliness! Your dignity! To begin with, dignity is a masculine defect! You, you always you. All that demanding and moaning and sulking and brooding of yours is no more than a disguise for your eternal deficiency—the inability to possess! Pooh! and even Fi! Demanding, and always a little bit at a time!"

I could not repress a smile.

"A little bit? But I want everything! It's not *my* fault if . . ."

My familiar demon cut me short by slicing the air with the flat of his hand.

"*Your* fault! *You* again! I said a *little bit* because all you wanted of Jean was his love. No, that isn't 'quite a tall order'! You spend your time putting Jean *opposite* you. That's the attitude of coition, no more. But it's another thing to inhabit him, to take him inside you! To take him inside you to the point where his radiance, his warmth, his manifestations of gaiety, anger, suffering, sensuality no longer appear to you as *someone else's,* but as the result of sublimest, most arrogant error, as the projections of your own innermost feelings! Does that bovine expression on your countenance indicate comprehension?"

"Yes . . . wait, Masseau, I'll put it another way: I'm in the dark but it doesn't frighten me, if I'm the one who's carrying the lantern? Is that it?"

"That's a faint, rough approximation."

"But . . . what about him, Masseau?"

"What do you mean, him?"

"I mean, will he do the same for me? Ought he to carry me inside him, as you say, to such a point that, for example, if he found me in the arms of another man, he'd exclaim: "Ah, how passionately that emanation of myself . . . loves!"

"That's none of your business. Such things don't concern you at all. As if feminine love had any connection with ours!"

"Ours . . ." He rocked to and fro on one foot, like a plucked heron. Yet this creature who looked so little like a man was speaking of love with emphatic authority.

"Woman, if the love you devote to your lover engages him in any way whatever towards you, it is no longer genuine love."

"What you're demanding of me in that case, Masseau, is mother-love."

"No," said Masseau. "The maternal instinct does not progress. It is born instantaneously—complete, fully armed and bleeding. Whereas love has the gift of tending towards its own perfection."

"Is that a piece of advice?"

"It is only an opinion. But it is based on observation."

"Frankly, you can't often have met her, this ideal female."

"Often, no. Only once. Therefore I married her. She was my housekeeper."

"So let us sing: 'He hath exalted the humble!'."

"I leave that sort of facile cynicism to you, my dear. You ought to go down on your knees and pray the good God that I wasn't mistaken when I judged you and Jean to be 'humble' enough to make a united couple. You, thank heaven, are not a genius and maybe Jean will never have his picture in the papers. You dream of obeying, on condition that you're allowed to go off all by yourself, with a great air of independence, to buy haberdashery at the Louvre. He likes to command, provided he is protected. In fact, you were— and how I regret having to employ that past tense!— you were both of you ordinary enough to engender a marvellous love."

A marvellous love! All those words he had spoken to me were the words of a man. It was all very intelligent, too intelligent for me. Instead of following his thought along the lines he suggested, I stopped short at the practical aspect of his discourse. I spoilt it by searching for a *recipe*, by trying to detect in it my lover's covert wishes. I reduced Masseau once more to his inferior status of messenger and in the admirable feminine self-sacrifice he proposed to me I saw only a means of luring Jean back.

⦗ 13 ⦘

THE SUN IS GOING DOWN INTO THE ISLAND-DOTTED sea. No aftercrop has grown in the meagre field that ends up as a beach and the trees in the copse blaze red in this rainless autumn. All the fresh colours of the landscape, red, grass-green, flaming pink, blue and mauve seem to be gathered together in the sea and in the clear sky it reflects.

A healthy tiredness has kept me sitting here on the terrace since lunch. The off-land breeze brings me the smell of meadows and burning weeds. It will not be long before Jean comes back. He will be carrying some sea-bird, hanging by its limp claws and swaying its slender dead neck. In spite of his scratched leggings and his faded old jacket, there will be something slightly unconvincing about this handsome hunter's appearance, as if he were only playing at being a sportsman. I shall receive his smile of greeting; I shall also receive his swift glance that will search out anything amiss in me and my surroundings; for example, this little coffee-stain on my white dress and the colchicums I gathered this morning lying fading on a bench.

The fact that we have been living together again for the past two months is a miracle which I humbly accept, as one must accept any prodigy, without seeking for an explanation. When I was a child, I was given a tree-frog which, instead of being green, was blue, and when I asked "But *why* is it blue?" the reply was: "Nobody knows. It's a prodigy."

He did not want to come back to me and I felt myself gradually dwindling away. I was already regretting my own death. I told myself: "What a pity! It would be better if some other human creature perished. There is still no much vigour in me; this body here, the brain behind this forehead—it is all good and sound, it could all be happy and useful."

But one day my sadness entered into a phase of compulsive activity, a blind, unreasoning determination: to see Jean again, to do everything possible to see him again, to have recourse to any conceivable means, to reject all calculations except those needed to work out an immediate, practical plan. The one I adopted was ingenuously simple: a pretended departure, then patient vigilance and, at the right moment, return.

A telephone call nearly ruined everything because once, knowing he had returned home, I yielded to the longing to hear his voice. In the booth at the hotel, I heard him exclaiming: "Hallo? . . . Well? . . . Who is that on the line?" and I stood silent, holding my breath as if the slightest movement would be fatal. He sensed it was I, for his voice changed register and I heard, in a lower tone: "Hallo, I say . . . Hallo . . ." Then he said hesitantly: "Is that . . ." and checked himself. And I heard nothing more but the sound of the receiver being hung up.

I had the connivance of Masseau and also, though not gratis, that of Victor the manservant. And I waited for Jean in his home one night, on the very day a letter from me, posted by Brague, assured him that I had gone to Le Havre where I was returning to my former profession.

I waited for him, with all the lights out, in our bedroom that was dimly illuminated by the gas lamp in the Boulevard Berthier. I listened to the passing hours striking, immune to weariness and fear, even to the fear that my romantic ambush might make me look ridiculous. No doubt, had I written to Jean: "I must speak to you", I should have seen him the next day but that was not the Jean I wanted.

I waited, conscious of a calm I had never known, as if I had reached the end of my life. I waited, sitting in the darkness. The scent of a rose tucked in my belt mounted insistently to my nostrils in the still air. I listened to the wheels of every car and to the sound of every footstep. And each time I said tranquilly: "It isn't he." Towards midnight I heard a slow footstep approaching, the footstep of a man who was not in any hurry, and my exquisite calm changed into a kind of madness. What should I do? Run away? Scream? Rush downstairs and open the door? Hide myself at the top of the house? I was on the point of doing any of them. And yet, when the same slow steps climbed the stairs, I was still sitting in the same place. I thought, as in a dream, that he might be frightened when he entered the room and, before he opened the door, I called out quite audibly: "Jean!"

He had certainly heard but he did not answer. He came in, closed the door behind him, turned on the light and we found ourselves standing face to face, shading our eyes with our hands.

"So here you are!" he said, after a moment.

"Here I am. I called out to you so that you wouldn't be too surprised to find me."

"Then this is an ambush?"

He broke into quiet laughter and I began to despair because he looked so affable, so carelessly at ease, as if he were paying a call. He seemed to me taller and handsomer and not so young as my memory pictured him. I was thinking, as far as I remember, on three different planes: first, he is there, before my eyes. Then: before the night is over, I shall know my fate. Finally: he already has two lines ruled on his forehead, he is not a child, he is not a cruel adolescent, he is a man, he is a being of my own kind and my own age, there must be means of communicating, of *treating* with him on a human basis.

I smiled too, and I said: "Why of course! With my old instinct for theatrical situations, what else would you expect?"

Something descended from his forehead and down over his whole face, a brutal shadow that was the forerunner of anger, but he pulled himself together and invited me to sit down. And, as he thrust out his hand to me, I took that hand and shook it gaily.

"Good evening, Jean."

"Good evening . . ."

On his face I could read deep perplexity and, at the same time, relief to find me gay—no tears, no dramatic cries, no threats. I was concentrating so hard on what I *ought* to do that it seemed to me I hardly loved him any more. I had entirely ceased to suffer. He sat down and ran his hand over his forehead.

"You look tired, Jean."

"Yes, just fancy, I'm working now. My father will never be able to go back to the office. I haven't acquired the habit of work—or the taste for it—yet. It's rather like being kept in to do an impot at school. I don't know why I'm telling you all this; it doesn't interest you in the least."

Behind the deliberately detached tone there was already reproach. At last reproach, at last the prelude to a lover's scene. I took my cue promptly.

"But it does interest me, Jean; it interests me very much, like everything else that concerns you."

I had spoken my line with too much conscious care; he saw the path I was trying to lure him into and dropped the subject. After this tactless blunder of mine, there was a quarter-of-an-hour of commonplaces and forced politenesses. The late hour, the unwonted light thrown through the wide-open window on to a scorched tree in the avenue, above all our unspoken thoughts gave this imbecile dialogue between a gentleman in evening dress and a lady in a tailor-made suit a hue of tragedy. I did not weary—"Dignity is a masculine defect", and it was Jean who gave the first signs of fatigue. He yawned nervously and, far from offending me, that yawn conjured up a Jean I had disdained to know—a serious Jean, at work, his plump, greedy man's neck bent over a page full of figures. His greedy man's neck . . . A savage sensuality suddenly burst up my innermost depths, sending the blood rushing up to my throat, making me cough, throbbing in my ears like a drum. It was the blind, primitive instinct of the animal crying frenziedly for its master. I know that, at that moment, I sprang to my feet, that the violence of my movement overturned my chair and that I said furiously: "So then?"

He had risen too; and, having seen my face, he was watching my hands.

"You're wrong," I said curtly. "Don't be frightened. I only meant to say: 'So then it's finished? It's finished, us two?' "

He looked at me sombrely, resenting most of all that I was forcing him to reply.

"What do you mean, finished? What do you mean, finished? Haven't you had enough of this existence? Did you find it funny, our life? You want to start all over again?"

At last our positions had been logically reversed; he was the one who talked, the one who complained and accused, all I had to do now was to listen, while inwardly answering with my whole heart: "Start all over again, oh yes! Start again, no matter how, provided it's with you." All I did was to slip in an occasional "But, Jean . . ." to make him go on, to make him sweep it aside like a river surging over some obstacle too feeble to dam it.

He was pacing up and down the bedroom.

"Start that existence all over again. I certainly beg your pardon if I have hurt you in any way," he said, with a venomous expression. "But I think we're quits."

"You feel bitter against me, Jean?"

He stopped still, as if to defy me.

"Yes, I feel bitter against you. I can't deny it. I can't even say whether I'm right or wrong, but I feel bitter against you."

"My darling . . ."

Low as I murmured it, he heard. But he grasped too that I was staggering with gratitude under this resentment that made me his again. The meek, cringing gratitude of a bullied wife, May's beaming face after he had knocked her about! In his turn, he undeceived me and said craftily: "No. You are free. But if it satisfies what you called in your letter your 'dignity as a woman', let me tell you you are the worst memory of my love life."

I had sat down again, and leaning my head against

the familiar silk of the armchair, I kept muttering, with closed eyes: "Yes . . . talk . . . talk . . ."

" 'Talk'! It's high time! After months of superior silence, now you say to me: 'Talk'! You boast of *listening to me think:* what need have you of my talking to you?"

"Oh, Jean! Listening to you think. . . . I might have said that in fun but . . ."

"Don't lie!" he shouted. "You're lying! You did listen to me thinking, or rather you attributed thoughts to me that conformed to the false idea you built up for yourself not of me, but of *man, man,* your enemy, your *bête noire.*"

"Yes . . . go on talking."

"The best I gave you—in the physical sense—only served you as a pretext to insult me the more. You conferred on me the merits of a boor and the deficiencies of an imbecile! Ah! did you think you were the only one of the two of us who heard the other thinking?"

He moved away to pour himself out a glass of water and I heard the neck of the water-jug rattling against the rim of the glass. I did not stir, I did not open my eyes for fear of stopping him. But, mercifully, he had not finished.

"And even if your Delphic priestess's vanity had not been constantly in the wrong, even if I had been the shifty swine you married once and for all long ago, listening to me think is a perpetual offence against my mental peace, against my security as an intelligent being, against the sacred imperviousness to which I have a right and which you ought not to violate!"

I did not open my eyes. I gently nodded my head, inwardly saying approvingly: "That's good. That's very good. And, besides, he had said: 'You ought not to' and not 'You ought not to have'."

He fell silent and I looked at him admiringly again, as he paced to and fro, palpitating with a resentment of which I was beginning to feel proud. "To take him inside you, to carry him inside you to the point where his radiance no longer appears to you as *someone else's.*"

"But, Jean, why didn't you defend yourself? Why didn't you explain yourself, reveal yourself?"

He rounded on me as if he were going to hit me.

"Defend myself! Explain myself? Judge's words, d'you hear? Judge's words after a judge's silence! To begin with, why me and not you?"

I rejoiced in that childish expression, like a thwarted schoolboy's. In any case I was rejoicing at being where I was, in the full spate of a lover's quarrel and that this one looked like lasting a long time.

"Fair enough," I said loyally.

He had seated himself on a little sofa and made no attempt to hide all the weariness on his face. Not once, since I had been there, had he had a lustful impulse; there had been not one of those vindictive kisses that had been our only language. As if he were thinking the same thing, he let fall these despondent words: "It's so meaningless, just going to bed together."

And I was not offended that, in my presence, he had reverted to an innocent being who wanted nothing from a woman except perhaps feminine warmth, the still, living shelter of two cradling arms. But that I dared not offer and it seemed to me only too certain that I would never dare to again.

"Is it true that you're going away again?" he asked in the same tired voice. "That you're returning to the stage, to your former profession?"

I shook my head.

"No, Jean, it isn't true. It's just one more lie. I haven't got a profession any more."

And, in my mind, I continued with sad sincerity: "I no longer have one, and there no longer exists any profession for me. There is only one aim in my life and it is there in front of me—this man who does not desire me and whom I love. To capture him, to tremble for fear of his escaping, to see him escape, to stalk him again patiently and recapture him—henceforth that is my only profession, my only mission in life. Then everything I loved before him will be restored to me; light, music, the whispering of trees, the shy, ardent appeal of tame animals, the proud silence of suffering men—all these will be restored to me, but *through* him and provided only I possess him. He seemed so near to me, so closely coupled to me that I thought I did possess him. I foolishly wanted to surmount him, taking him for an obstacle when, in fact, he was the limit of my universe. I think many women, at the outset, make the same mistake as I did, before they resume their right place which is *on this side* of a man."

"Then what do you propose to do?"

I tried to put all my reply in a look, but his eyes refused mine as definitely as if he were saying: "No, no, it's too soon." His expression, at that moment, was excessively severe as if he wanted to discourage me for good and all. I nearly smiled; he did not know I had all the rest of my life in which to wait.

"What am I going to do? That's going to depend a little on you, Jean, and when I say *a little* . . . I'm going to begin by leaving you to get some sleep, because it's late and you're working."

I had picked up the very ancient, half worn-away jade fruit and I was fondling it as I looked round for another trace of my passage through this bedroom. I caressed its cold, smooth surface, then I slipped it into my handbag.

"Aren't you going to say anything to me, Jean?"

His eyes followed my hands, aware of their symbolic gesture of taking back, of departing.

"Goodbye, my silent one."

Standing there, I felt my confidence and my stubborn resolution on the verge of collapse, like my body. I secured my hat more firmly to leave, saying to myself: "He's going to let me go. But I haven't gone yet. I'll cling to any straw. I haven't gone yet."

He had stood up too and towered above me. I raised my eyes and I was seized with an odd feeling of extreme respect for myself, for the woman I was a few weeks ago, the Renée of last season, the woman who had had this man.

"My silent one, you never speak and you write even less. You've left me in such silence."

He lowered his brow and he averted that suddenly evasive glance that made him less beautiful.

"What did you want me to do? Answer your letter, write more scenes, exchange abominable words one doesn't forget? At a moment when neither of us could tolerate each other a moment longer, put more poison between us?"

"It's true that . . ." I conceded slavishly. But I was thinking: "I know very well that he isn't perfect. If fate gives him back to me, I shall often see that thieving animal's smile of his again, that recoil from a painful truth, from having to make an effort. I know very well that, before giving a little of himself, he is capable of demanding everything of me while gracefully apologising for not demanding more. But since, just as he is, I find in vulgar parlance 'as good as I'll get' and since I have neither the wish nor the right to belong to a hero, my imperfect self wants this imperfect Jean and none other."

"Then, au revoir, Jean?"

I held out my hand, and, as he bent down to kiss it, I saw the charming cleft in his upper lip quiver under his nostrils. I hesitated only a second: I must get him back, no matter by what means. I must gain time! I must throw him down, along with myself, not this time to drain and exhaust each other but to try and make a clear jet spring up out of the mud of our sad, sombre sensuality—the pure jet of love of which we might one day be worthy.

And, as a beginning, I ran a swift, caressing finger over his delicate ear. He started and turned away, with the gesture of a tempted woman.

"My darling . . ."

He shook his head, and warned me in a dull voice: "Take care! Once more, it's only desire."

His gaze took possession again of what he found attractive in me; my shoulders, my bosom, my hands which were clasped so as not to caress him too hastily.

"I tell you—do you hear?—that it's only desire!"

I nodded to signify, "Yes, I know."

The hand of my master fell heavily on me.

"Is that enough for you? Is that enough for you? Is that all you want of me? Is that all you bring me?"

Too exhausted to lie, I threw myself into his arms

and I closed my eyes so that he should not see that it was my soul I was giving him.

The sun is going down and drawing out the conical shadow of the reefs over the sea. An hour has passed and I am still here under the canvas awning, against the sun-gilded wall. Over there, very far away, on the top of a jagged cliff is a tiny figure which moves capriciously; now coming closer, now stopping, now going away again. It is he. He too can see my white dress. He will come without hurrying himself, since I am waiting for him. Only when I see him down there, dark and clear-cut on the pale yellow beach, shall I get up and go down to meet him. I shall not hurry either, since he will be coming towards me. He will put his arm round my shoulder and say it has been a splendid day, he will tell me about the birds he went after, about the ferret that escaped. We shall exchange few words, because all our words enrich us with a little more of each other.

He will go off again tomorrow, anxious to enjoy every hour he can of this countryside he loves during his brief holiday. Here, he walks strenuously and displays the energy of a contented peasant. I follow his example, but in his wake and at a slower, gentler pace than my old one. It seems to me, as I watch him launch out enthusiastically into life, that he has changed places with me; that he is the eager vagabond and that I am the one who gazes after him, anchored for ever.

ABOUT THE AUTHOR

Sidonie Gabrielle Colette (1873–1954) was one of the most famous and honored French writers of this century. The first woman member of The Academie Goncourt, a holder of the Grand Cross of the Legion of Honor, she was also the first woman in French history to be granted a state funeral.

Colette began her writing career in collaboration with Willy, her husband. In 1900, when she was twenty-seven, Colette's first novel, *Claudine at School,* was published and became a sensational success. During the next few years, several *Claudine* books followed. After divorcing Willy, Colette earned her living as a music-hall mime, and in 1907, her first independent novel appeared, *Retreat from Love.*

With the outbreak of World War I, Colette began a career as a special correspondent in Rome and Venice and as a contributor to *Le Matin,* a leading Paris daily. Her journalism included dramatic criticism, law-court reporting, and sketches of contemporary life. During this time, Colette continued to write novels.

During her last years, Colette, crippled by arthritis and confined to her Paris apartment, wrote reminiscences and descriptive works that gained her new renown. Before her death in 1954, at the age of eighty-one, Colette had written more than fifty books and was best known as the creator of *Gigi, Cheri* and *The Last of Cheri,* and the *Claudine* novels. Her place in twentieth-century fiction is comparable among her countrymen only with that of Proust.

Books by Colette to be published by Ballantine are: *The Vagabond, The Shackle, Cheri* and *The Last of Cheri, Claudine at School, Claudine in Paris, Claudine Married* and *Claudine and Annie, The Pure and the Impure,* and *Letters from Colette.*